FRIENDS
AND
ENEMIES

FRIENDS
AND
ENEMIES

BY LOUANN GAEDDERT

A Jean Karl Book

Atheneum Books for Young Readers

NEW YORK LONDON TORONTO SYDNEY SINGAPORE

Atheneum Books for Young Readers
An imprint of Simon & Schuster
Children's Publishing Division
1230 Avenue of the Americas
New York, New York 10020
Book design by Angela Carlino
The text of this book is set in Baskerville BE.
Printed in the United States of America
4   6   8   10   9   7   5
Library of Congress Cataloging-in-Publication Data
Gaeddert, LouAnn Bigge.
Friends and enemies / LouAnn Gaeddert.
p.   cm.
"A Jean Karl book."
Summary: In 1941 in Kansas, as America enters World War II,
fourteen-year-old William finds himself alienated from his friend Jim,
a Mennonite who does not believe in fighting for any reason and
refuses to support the war effort in any way.
ISBN 0-689-82822-5
1. World War, 1939-1945–United States–Juvenile fiction. [1. World War, 1939-1945–United
States–Fiction. 2. War–Fiction. 3. Pacifism–Fiction.
4. Friendship–Fiction. 5. Mennonites–Fiction. 6. Kansas–Fiction.] I. Title.
PZ7.G118Fr   2000
[Fic]–dc21
99-19143

ATHENEUM BOOKS FOR YOUNG READERS
BY LOUANN GAEDDERT

Breaking Free

Hope

Friends and Enemies

I wish to thank the following people who have helped me in so many ways:

All the Mennonites who shared their memories of World War II with me.

The professors and staff of Bethel College, the Mennonite Archives, and the Kauffman Museum, all located in North Newton, Kansas.

The staffs of the public library in Hutchinson, Kansas and the Berkshire Athenaeum in Pittsfield, Massachusetts.

My husband's Goering cousins in and around Pretty Prairie, Kansas.

Finally, I wish to express my love and appreciation to my husband's mother, Ida Gaeddert.

FRIENDS AND ENEMIES

Chapter 1

I met Jim Reimer on the day we moved from Topeka in eastern Kansas to Plaintown in the south-central part of the state. It was Saturday, August 30, 1941. The next day I met Clive Van Dyne. I knew from the beginning which one would be my friend.

Jim was walking down Main Street with his dad while I was straining and sweating, trying to lift my end of Mom's sewing machine up the front steps toward my dad. I wasn't a very big fourteen-year-old. Truth? I was short and skinny, some said *puny*.

"We'll just wait for one of the men." Dad was referring to two members of our old church who were helping us move from Topeka to Plaintown.

"Out of the way, lad," boomed a voice from behind me.

I stepped back into what felt like a padded wall

and looked up—and up—into a face deeply tanned and weathered with squint lines around bright blue eyes, the face of a farmer.

"Name's Dick Reimer. My boy, Jim." He nodded toward the boy beside him and hoisted the sewing machine up the steps toward my dad.

"I'm Bill Spencer," Dad said, panting. "Tomorrow I'll be the Methodist minister, but today I'm a moving man. This is my son, William. Are you members of my new congregation?"

"No, we just happened to be on Main Street running a few Saturday morning errands. We're Mennonites, but glad to welcome you to Plaintown. Where do you want this machine?"

Dad and Mr. Reimer carried the sewing machine through the front door and up the steep steps to the second floor. I picked up two chairs, to demonstrate that I wasn't all *that* weak. Jim picked up two others. We carried them through the narrow hall and living room into the dining room.

Beside his father, Jim had looked small; beside me, he was a Goliath, a lanky Goliath. Jim's eyes are even bluer than his father's. His left eyebrow is arched like most eyebrows, but his right eyebrow slants up toward his temple and then drops straight down. That eyebrow makes him look surprised. Always.

"Do you live near here?" I asked.

"Farm."

"Way out in the country or just a little way?"

"Three miles."

Obviously, Jim wasn't much of a talker. Anything I wanted to know I'd have to ask. "Where do you go to school?"

"Here. High School. First year."

"Me, too." I felt a laugh bubbling up into my throat. "I'll sure be glad to know somebody on the first day of school. We've already moved twice since I started kindergarten. Comes with being a preacher's kid, but we won't move again while I'm in high school. Dad's promised. Mom made him promise. She hates to move." I clamped my mouth shut. I shouldn't have mentioned my mother, who had disappeared as soon as we'd arrived.

"Yoo-hoo." A large woman with skinny legs and red shoes entered the hall through the open door and waddled on into the living room. "I've had my girl bake this little cake to welcome our new minister and his family to Plaintown." She stretched her neck to try to see through the dining room into the kitchen beyond.

"Thank you. This looks delicious. I know we'll enjoy it." I took the cake from her hands. It was huge, probably three layers, and covered with swirls of chocolate. I'm polite because I'm the preacher's kid. If I'm rude, someone is sure to complain to my parents. I often wish that my father had a different job.

The lady walked back to the hall and looked up the stairs. "Where *is* your mother?" she squawked.

"Oh, she's here somewhere." I stretched my lips

into a broad smile. My smile turned real as I thought how much this woman looked like a goose. "Mom's probably keeping my sisters out of the way of the moving men."

The goose-lady sighed. "I expected to make a few suggestions about the arrangement of the furniture. I hadn't realized your mother would be bringing pieces of her own. That small chair is quite attractive."

I wondered what suggestions she might make for changing the shape of the couch from lumpy or the color from dirty brown. If this woman wanted to please my mother, she'd hack the couch into small pieces and burn it.

I should explain that a minister's family usually lives in a house owned by the church. The Plaintown parsonage is shaped like a cracker box, small and tall with the narrow side facing the street. At least it's white; our parsonage in Topeka had been painted dark, dismal green. Parsonages usually come furnished with other people's castoffs. We're lucky to have some furniture Grandma gave us when she moved out of her big house. Mom says that Grandma's furniture is what makes any house our home.

"Mother will be sorry to have missed you," I said, crossing my fingers behind my back.

"Tell your mother that Mrs. Van Dyne, Mrs. Arthur C. Van Dyne, brought this cake. Tell her I look forward to meeting her at church tomorrow." When she reached the door, she turned back. "Perhaps we can find something to replace that couch. I hadn't realized how worn it had become. The last preacher allowed his children to jump on it. I hope you children will be more considerate of church property."

Jim had disappeared, but when the click of Mrs. Van Dyne's high heels had faded, he reappeared carrying two boxes of books. I took the top one, amazed that Jim could manage *two* such heavy boxes.

"Missus Van Busybody," he muttered as we stacked the boxes in front of the chairs in the dining room.

"I think she looks like a goose. Do you?"

"Yeah." Jim grinned. "Mrs. Busybody Van Goose."

"How old is the gosling who made this cake?"

"'Bout sixty." Jim's eyes twinkled.

"That's impossible. Missus Busybody isn't sixty. Her girl—"

"Housekeeper. Mrs. Hanson. Widow of a farmer. Lost their farm to Van Dyne's bank. Nice lady. Great cakes."

"So shall we give this cake the taste test?"

We went to the kitchen and set the cake on the chipped metal table. I cut the first two wedges of cake and then four more when our dads and the two men from our old church appeared, as if by magic. Minutes later most of the cake had been eaten, and the men were ready to leave.

I stood on the porch beside my dad as he thanked each person. "We'll miss all our old friends," he said to the men who were about to drive back to Topeka in their truck.

Amen, I said to myself. I was sure going to miss my Topeka buddies, Jack and George and Pinky and Pete. The five of us had hung around together during all of the four years I had lived in Topeka. They were the reason I hated to be moving to Plaintown.

"We're glad to have new friends," Dad said to the Reimers.

Amen, I said again. I would certainly welcome the sight of that crazy eyebrow among the sea of strange faces on the first day of school!

After our lunch Dad took Maggie, age six, upstairs for a nap. He took a sandwich, a cup of tea, and the last piece of busybody cake with him—for Mom, who must have been hiding in one of the bedrooms.

Dad and I and my ten-year-old sister, Darlene, spent the afternoon greeting the people who came to the door with food.

"Manna from heaven!" Dad exclaimed over cakes and casseroles and Jell-O salads. After he'd said the same thing about three times, Darlene and I began mouthing the words whenever the doorbell rang. He must have seen us, because he stopped and just thanked the people. Our dad sprinkles Bible verses and Bible stories into every conversation. It's embarrassing. Between deliveries we unpacked books and put them on the shelves Dad had set up in the dining room.

It was dinnertime before Mom finally appeared. She went right to the kitchen and lifted the waxed paper from some of the pies and cakes on the metal table. Then she peered into the packed icebox, lifting the covers from some of the bowls and pans.

"It hadn't occurred to me that we wouldn't have a refrigerator. But I guess we should be grateful that someone thought to have ice delivered." She sighed. "So which of the three tuna fish casseroles shall we eat tonight?"

"Fried chicken," we shouted in unison.

"My choice, too." She laughed. "We'll have tuna fish tomorrow—and Monday and Tuesday. If anyone asks you how you liked whatever she brought, what will you say?"

"It was just delicious. Thank you *sooo* much." Darlene spoke with a gooey-sweet voice.

"Perfect." Mom kissed Darlene's cheek.

"You want us to lie?" I asked.

Mom smiled at me. "Yes, William, I do—in this one instance."

When we went upstairs after supper, the doors were all open. Mom had not been wasting time while she was hiding. Our beds were made and turned back so that they looked welcoming. My model airplanes were laid out on the double bed that took up most of my room. Mom picked up the string and tacks and scissors she'd put on the chest of drawers and announced that we'd hang them right then.

Darlene was pouting because she wanted a room of her own. I didn't blame her. My little room had dirty beige wallpaper with huge pink roses, but I'd rather have it all to myself than have to share with Maggie and her dolls and her stuffed animals.

The next morning, the bell in the squat tower of the Plaintown Methodist Church rang to announce that Sunday school was about to begin. Just that once we didn't have to go to Sunday school. An hour later it rang again to call the congregation to church. Mom stood on the little porch outside the front door and checked us out as we left the house to walk along the sidewalk to the church next door.

You should have seen us. Darlene, who usually wore braids, had slept with her hair rolled up in rags so she could have curls for this special Sunday. Her hair is the same color as mine, a boring light brown. Our eyes are also light brown. She'd been standing ever since she'd put on her Sunday dress so that it would not have one wrinkle when she walked down the aisle.

I'd had a haircut just before we left Topeka, and my cowlick was slicked down, at least for the moment. I was wearing my suit, even though it was ninety degrees in the shade. I don't usually wear it in hot weather, and I'd hoped to have outgrown it over the summer. No such luck. Mom said it was perfect with the cuffs turned down. She also said I could take off my jacket when we reached our pew.

Maggie's hair is always curly and blond. People say she looks like Shirley Temple. She was wearing a pink dress with ruffles.

When we reached the church doors, Mom

straightened her new hat—which sat on top of her head like a pancake. Then she straightened her shoulders, took Maggie's hand, and glided down the center aisle. She turned left and right, smiling at the people in the pews. She reminded me of a queen greeting her subjects. Darlene and I plastered our Sunday smiles on our faces and walked behind her, staring straight ahead.

The aisle of this church is longer than the aisle in our Topeka church, and there is a balcony. The pews were packed. Everyone was out to see the new minister and his family. We stepped into the third pew from the front and, having made my "first impression," I took off my jacket.

You may be wondering why Mom hid from the people on moving day. For one thing, she was shy and she wilted like a flower without water when anyone criticized her or us. For another, she believed in first impressions. She didn't want to meet these people until we were all "presentable," which meant that our shoes were polished and our fingernails were clean. Another thing you should know: Mom is very kind. Dad says that her silence often helps folks more than his words.

This service was like most church services. We sang and prayed the prayer in the bulletin and read the responsive reading in the back of the hymnbook. The choir sang, the ushers took the offering, and Dad preached. During the service, Maggie drew pictures on the back of the bulletin, but Darlene and I were expected to sit with our hands folded in our laps.

I don't know what went on in Darlene's head, but I listened to the sermon just long enough to be able to say something when Dad asked me about it. This sermon was about welcoming change. The Pharisees wanted everything to stay the same, but Jesus said, "A new commandment I give unto you, that ye love one another." I knew that verse, so I began to think about planes.

I imagined flying over Germany dropping a bomb right on Hitler's headquarters and ending the war in Europe. I was planning to be a pilot. *Move over, Charley Lindbergh; make way for Will Spencer!*

I saw stunt flyers once. A lady with a long white scarf walked on the wing of the plane. A man climbed from the wing of one plane down a rope ladder to the wing of another plane. One plane did loops and came down so low it seemed it would crash into the ground before the nose turned up into the sky. I begged for five dollars so I could go up for five minutes. My father said we didn't have five dollars for such foolishness. My mother said that even if we had five dollars she wouldn't let me "risk my life."

While I sat in the third pew with my hands folded, I imagined what it must be like to fly up there with the birds. My thoughts weren't on heaven but they were above the clouds.

During the last verse of the closing hymn, Dad stepped down from the pulpit and waited for Mom to walk in front of him to the back of the church. He said the benediction from the back. He and Mom stood together at the door to shake hands with the people as they left.

Darlene and I each took one of Maggie's hands. Since we were so far front, it took us a very long time to get out. Soon we'd know a shortcut from the sanctuary to our yard, but this Sunday we had to wait.

I was wishing I could sit up in the balcony instead of in the third row when Mrs. Busybody Van Goose clasped my shoulder. I thanked her for the cake and turned to go on down the aisle.

Her fingernails dug into my shoulder. "I want you to meet someone I know will soon be your dear friend, my husband's brother's son, Clive Van Dyne. Clive, this very polite young man is William Spencer. He, too, will be a freshman in the high school, so I want you to help him get acquainted with the nicest children in town. Shake hands, boys."

Clive was even bigger than Jim, not taller but broader. *Were all the boys in Plaintown giants?* His skin and hair were almost white. His face was so round and his eyes so small and pale that he looked like the man-in-the-moon. I expected a limp handshake. Dumb me! The ring on his finger was turned so that it dug a hole in my hand as he squeezed like a boa constrictor.

It hurt, but I kept on smiling—which surprised him. I could tell. When his aunt turned to talk to someone else, he glared at me.

"Preacher's Brat," he muttered. "Wait till school starts; I'll get you then. You'll find out who's in charge." He ran off between the pews.

Darlene had gone on ahead with Maggie. She was at the back of the church talking with a girl about her age. At home Darlene rattled on and on about a new friend named Cynthia. Monday was Labor Day. School would start on Tuesday, but the day would end at noon so the teachers could attend meetings. Cynthia had invited Darlene and some other girls to come to her house for lunch on Tuesday. They planned to play Monopoly all afternoon.

"I'm glad to see that you made a friend at church, too, William," Dad said. "Mrs. Van Dyne says that her nephew will help you get acquainted."

A boa constrictor would be a better friend than Clive Van Dyne! I knew that already.

Chapter 2

We labored on Labor Day. After breakfast we moved some of the parsonage furniture down to the basement.

When Mom said, "I wish we could move that couch to the dump," I told her what Mrs. Van Dyne had said about replacing it and about the previous minister's children who had jumped on it. I said that Mrs. Van Dyne hoped we would be more careful of *church property.*

"Oh, dear. Is Mrs. Van Dyne another Trudy Tarbell?"

I groaned at the thought. Mom called Trudy Tarbell "the bane-of-my-existence." She was glad to leave her behind in Topeka.

After greeting Mom, Trudy would cough and then say, "You know, my dear, I would never interfere with our dear Pastor Spencer's lovely family." Then she'd suggest that Mom serve dinner earlier on nights when

Dad had meetings, or spank Maggie when she sucked her thumb, or insist that I say more than just "hello" to the older women in the church.

Dad said we should feel sorry for Trudy Tarbell because she had no family and was old and lonely. Mrs. Van Dyne had a family and she wasn't all that old. She even had a *girl* to do her baking. Still, it seemed likely that she would be another bane-of-Mom's-existence. Her nephew was already the bane of mine.

When we had finished moving the furniture, Darlene and I washed every dish that had been in the house when we arrived and every dish we had brought with us. Maggie dried the spoons. Mom scrubbed the kitchen cupboards and then the floor and finally hung yellow curtains at the windows and covered the church's chipped kitchen table with a yellow-checked cloth. "There," she said with satisfaction. "The kitchen is livable."

That night I lay on my back in the middle of the big sagging bed, property of the Methodist Church of Plaintown, Kansas, and asked God to arrange things so that Jim Reimer would be in my first class. Trying not to think of Clive's promise to *get* me, I rolled to one side of the bed and to the other side. I put two pillows under my head, then just one, then none. I was hot and sweaty and worried and edgy.

Not scared, I told myself while I was remembering the bully who had attacked me on my first day of school in

Topeka. Without any warning, he'd jumped me from behind and pulled me to the ground. I'd tried to fight back but I'd ended up with a bloody nose and bruised body.

It would have been worse if Jack and George and Pinky and Pete hadn't come along and pulled him off of me. Jack and George and Pinky and Pete had been my buddies from that day forward. *Jack and George and Pinky and Pete.* I said those four names over and over until, at last, I slept.

Tuesday morning Maggie ran into my room before the alarm went off and jumped on my bed. "Today I'm going to learn to read," she squealed.

"It takes months to learn to read," I muttered.

"Everybody learns to read in the first grade," she said in that sure-of-herself way she has.

"It takes more than one day, darling." Mom took her hand and led her back into the hall. "Time for you to be getting up, William."

I buried my face in one pillow and put the other pillow on top of my head. Still I could hear Darlene singing and Maggie chattering. Mom called to me as she went downstairs.

Dad came to the foot of the stairs. "'This is the day which the Lord hath made; and we will rejoice and be glad in it.'" That verse from Psalm 118 is one of Dad's favorites.

Finally, as I knew she would, Mom came and sat on my bed and lifted the pillow from my head. "Time to get up. I've brought your orange juice."

"I can't drink it. I'm sick." I moaned pitifully.

"I know. But you'll be just as sick tomorrow if you don't go today. Remember how you enjoyed school in Topeka."

I wanted to tell her about Clive, but I didn't. She would worry; she might even come to school to walk home with me. Nobody could survive that humiliation. So I kept quiet and thought about Jack and George and Pinky and Pete while I sat up and drank my juice.

"Don't forget your glasses," Mom said as she left the room. "You know where they are, don't you?"

They were just where I had put them, in the top drawer of my dresser. Although I hated to be seen in them and hadn't worn them since I left Topeka, I really liked what they did for my eyesight. It was amazing! I could read the blackboard from the back of the room. I could see the separate leaves on trees and read signs across the street. Putting on glasses for the first time last year was like the moment when the picture show starts in a dark theater. New shapes suddenly appear. If only the glasses didn't make me look like a bookworm, which I am but which I don't want to advertise.

Dad had offered to help me enroll, but walking to school with him would have been almost as humiliating as walking home with Mom. I went alone with a lump the size of a baseball in my chest. Groups of kids were clustered on the sidewalk and lawn in front of the high school, greeting one another, laughing. I pretended I couldn't see them as I went straight to the front doors.

During the few minutes it took me to find the principal's office, the lump in my chest grew. My hand shook as I handed my records from the Topeka school to the lady behind the counter. I don't remember anything the principal said. Too soon I was in the hall clutching my schedule of classes and room numbers.

By then the lump in my chest was the size of a basketball, pushing on my lungs so that my breath came in gasps. Nevertheless, I put on my nothing-worries-me face before I opened the door of my home room. *Jack and George and Pinky and Pete.* The eyes of every person at every desk turned to watch me walk to the front of the room. I gave some papers I had received in the principal's office to the teacher and took the only empty seat, which was directly in front of the teacher's desk.

She smiled at me, then turned to the class. "We'll need someone to show William around. It's the first day of high school for all of you, but you have been here for orientation—and for games and plays and concerts. William has just arrived from Topeka. He has brought a fine record of scholarship and behavior with him."

Her words made me sound like the kind of kid other kids hate. I wanted to crawl under my desk, but I listened while she told me there were fifty-eight freshmen in two homerooms and that they came from the town grade school and from three different country schools. "Who'll help William find his way around the building?"

Let Jim be sitting in the back of this room and let him volunteer, I begged silently.

"I'll show William around." The voice was not Jim's.

"How nice of you, Clive." The teacher smiled.

Several kids snickered, and I knew for sure that my first day of high school would be horrible. At least it would be short. Classes would each last about twenty minutes so that school would be over at noon. I would not have to endure a lunch hour.

On the way to our algebra class Clive introduced me to about six guys. "This here's the Preacher's Brat," he said, "But we'll call him Silly Willy."

"Hello, Silly Willy." Each one of them guffawed and punched me on the arm or the back.

We received our algebra books and a homework assignment. Then gym.

"Won't be hard to find the dressing room," Clive said. "Down the main staircase and turn left. First door on the left."

I followed his instructions and was about to push open the first door on the left when I was surrounded by girls—older girls, probably juniors or seniors. They laughed while red heat crept up from my collar to my neck and across my face.

I was looking for a pathway through the girls when one of them stepped aside to let me pass. "This is the door to the girls' dressing room," she whispered. "The double doors lead into the gym. The boys' dressing room is the next door after the gym doors."

Jim was in my gym class, and so was every other

freshman boy, including the bane-of-my-existence, nephew of Busy-body Van Goose!

Jim and I had English together, and history, and then band. Jim plays the trumpet; I play the sax.

I didn't meet up with Clive again until the last class of the day, biology. During the walk back to our homeroom, Clive pointed to his ring, a heavy weapon, gold with fancy letters on a black stone. When I looked into his face, he nodded and smirked. *Wait till we get outside.* That was his message.

I went to the boys' bathroom. Clive followed me. Back in the hall I stopped to tie my shoe. He waited. He walked beside me out into the hot, bright sunlight. Other boys joined us. I said my magic words faster and faster: *Jack and George and Pinky and Pete. Jack 'n' George 'n' Pinky and Pete. Jack George Pinky Pete. JackGeorgePinky . . .*

"Hi, William." Jim came up on the other side of me, and together we walked away from the school and from Clive. When we got to the sidewalk, Jim nodded toward a tall boy leaning against a black Model T. "Brother Phil," he said.

Phil was taller and broader than Jim, but he had the same bright blue eyes and wide mouth. He was talking with a girl in a blue dress with a blue ribbon in her golden hair.

"Hello, William," she said as we approached. *How could she know my name?* She explained in the next sentence: "I'm in the Methodist Church choir. I watched you during the sermon. I admire the way you can sit so still. I wondered what you were thinking about." She laughed. "I'll bet it wasn't the sermon."

I hadn't seen her in the choir because I hadn't been wearing my glasses.

"I won't tell anyone." She laughed again. "If I was wondering what you were thinking, I couldn't have been listening very hard either, could I?" She turned back to look up at Phil. She kissed her own fingers and patted his cheek with them. "See you tomorrow."

I turned toward home, and there was Clive standing about six feet from me, with four other boys.

"Hop in," Phil said. "Won't be out of our way to drive by the parsonage."

I didn't have to be asked twice.

"Clive a problem?" Jim asked.

I just nodded. I couldn't admit I was scared of Clive.

The Reimers drove me home; I had escaped Clive once, but I knew I couldn't escape him forever.

On Wednesday Clive started calling me Silly Willy Four-Eyes, which *he* thought was very funny. His friends did, too. Twice he came up behind me and whispered, "Today's the day. Just you wait."

I walked from history to the lunchroom with Jim and sat with him. He introduced me to some of the guys sitting near us. One was his cousin. Most had gone to the country school near the Reimer farm. Clive and other guys from our class sat at another table. After lunch we all shot baskets in the school yard.

Several times I noticed Clive glaring at me. His little faded eyes in his doughy white face looked evil. Once he held up his right hand and pointed to his ring with his other hand—just to be sure I'd know that he was still wearing it.

At the end of the school day Clive walked with me from biology back to our homeroom. "Coward," he sneered. "You think you can hide behind that big Mennonite farmer forever? They talk German, just like Hitler."

"Jim doesn't talk German," I said.

"Bet he does at home. All Mennonites talk German. They're spies for Hitler."

"That's dumb!" I said, which was probably a dumb thing for me to say to the big guy who had promised to *get* me.

"You'll find out who's dumb." As we entered the homeroom door, he stomped down hard on the top of my foot.

When I walked out of the school, trying not to limp, I saw Clive and his pals waiting on the sidewalk. I looked for Phil's car; it was just where it had been the day before, but Phil wasn't near it, nor was Jim. I considered my options. I could go back into the school, but Clive and company wouldn't leave until I came out, and I couldn't stay in the school forever. I could go the opposite direction, but they could run after me.

I did what I had to do. First I put on my glasses; some

guys are afraid to hit a guy with glasses. I felt like the Cowardly Lion, but I curled my lip and swaggered toward them, hoping I looked like Gary Cooper.

As soon as I stepped onto the sidewalk outside of the school grounds, Clive shoved his hand into my chest so that my swagger became a stagger.

"Don't hit a guy with glasses," one of Clive's pals shouted.

"What? And let him get away?" He hit me again, with his fist. I got one good punch in his fat belly, and then I was down on the ground. He stopped hitting for just a minute and tried to yank my glasses off of my face, but the wires were wrapped around my ears. "Take 'em off yourself, Silly Willy Four-Eyes," he snarled. "Then I'll show you who's is charge around here."

Slowly, I loosened the wire around one ear at a time while Clive held the opposite arm. Somebody took my glasses from me, and Clive began pummeling me on every part of my upper body. I struggled and kicked and got a few punches on his shoulders, and one on his cheek that made him howl. And then I was on the receiving end of a burst of blows.

"That's enough, Clive. Cut it out." I didn't recognize the voice. Clive didn't stop. A hand reached out and grabbed one of Clive's fists. Another hand was reaching for his other fist.

At the same time, Jim yelled, "Stop that. Right now."

Clive used his still free hand to deliver a blow that made me want to howl.

"You should know that bullies and friends of bullies won't be allowed to try out for the basketball team." Jim again, speaking softly and calmly as if he were just passing on a bit of interesting information.

"His brother's the captain of the team," someone whispered.

"And president of the student body," another guy added.

Both of Clive's hands were being held by a tall guy with red hair and freckles who pulled Clive off of me. By the time Jim had pulled me to my feet, Clive and most of the spectators were halfway down the block.

The redhead stood in front of me with his head bowed. "I'm sorry about . . ." He shrugged his shoulders and loped away before I could thank him for removing Clive.

Another boy stepped forward and handed me my glasses. "Name's Barry. I wouldn't have let Clive hurt you."

I couldn't help laughing; Barry was even smaller than me. I thanked him just the same. Then I thanked Jim. "Where's your brother?" I asked. We were standing near the Model T.

"Meeting. I'll walk with you."

"I'll see Clive doesn't hit him again." Barry grinned at both of us. "I pass the parsonage on the way home. I'll take care of Sill . . . William."

Jim nodded, but he continued to walk with us, past the church and up the steps to our house. Mother called from the kitchen and, when she saw Jim and Barry, she cut us each a big slab of another of the cakes someone had brought us on Saturday and poured us glasses of milk.

When we had finished, Jim thanked my mom. "Phil's waiting," he said as he headed for the front door. "See you tomorrow, William."

Barry thanked my mom and left by our back door.

"Into the bathtub," Mom said as soon as they were gone.

My cheek had been bleeding but was scabbing over. My rib cage hurt. Bruises and bumps were beginning to appear on my chest and my arms. Otherwise, I wasn't hurt much, thanks to Jim—and the redhead.

Chapter 3

The next morning, Barry was sitting on our front steps. He jumped up and bounced on the balls of his feet while he told me how easy it was for him to come by for me. His house faced the next street, so he just walked through his backyard, down the alley, and through our backyard.

It felt good to have Barry chattering along beside me. He said that he'd been born in Plaintown. His dad was in California but would be coming home soon. He and his little brother and mother went to our church.

We had turned off Main Street onto Center Street, which leads to the high school, when a loud through-the-teeth whistle pierced the air. It was Clive. Who would have thought he could whistle like that?

"Hey, Gnat, get yourself over here," he growled.

Barry waved to Clive and took a step toward the street and then a step back toward me. "I'll tell him you want to walk with us, too. Okay, William?"

"Don't." *How could he think I'd walk on the same block with Clive?*

"Move," the bully commanded.

Barry looked at me—and then at Clive. "Tomorrow, maybe," he whispered as he turned and dashed across the street.

I walked on alone, kicking a rock ahead of me and wishing I were back in Topeka. I ate lunch with Jim and his friends and walked home alone. Friday was the same as Thursday.

Saturdays in Topeka I had raced through my chores, cleaning my room, changing my sheets, and emptying the wastebaskets. My record time for all three jobs was nineteen minutes. I had spent the rest of the day with Jack and George and Pinky and Pete. If it wasn't raining we went to the school yard or the park and played ball. After lunch we went to the picture show.

My first Saturday in Plaintown I dawdled through my chores; there was no reason to hurry. Then I mowed the lawn. After lunch I dragged myself to the library and checked out a copy of *Great Expectations,* which we had to read for English, and a copy of *The Yearling,* which Pinky said was a good story. On the way back with my books, I walked across the street from the movie house, the Roxy.

"Hey, Silly Willy, you only got two eyes today. How you going to see the movie?" Clive, of course.

"I saw that movie in Topeka, last spring. It's lousy." I hurried on, feeling angry—and sad. It *was* a lousy movie. Of course I didn't want to see it again. *I wouldn't have gone if Clive had asked me,* I told myself. He looked like a giant slug and he was mean. There was only one thing to admire about Clive: his whistle. I wished I could whistle through my teeth.

Back at the parsonage I turned the pages of the new issue of *LIFE* magazine and listened to a ball game and tried to whistle like Clive. I couldn't. I felt mighty sorry for myself. Mom felt sorry for me, too. I could tell by the way she patted my shoulder.

Clive was in my Sunday school class; so was the redheaded guy, whose name was Allen, and Barry. I recognized two other guys who ate lunch with Clive and who were with him on Saturday at the Roxy. Their names were Tom and John. It would take me a couple of weeks to remember the names of the other guys and the girls in the class.

After Sunday school was church. The pretty girl with the golden hair sang a solo. I checked the bulletin and saw that her name was Anne Armstrong. I saw her again at the youth group meeting that evening. Barry was there, too, and Allen and about twenty other high school kids, but not Clive.

I wondered if Barry's mother made him go to the youth group. I had to go every week; minister's kids have to *set an example*. I usually had to go to evening church after the youth group meeting, too. Do I like spending four hours in church every Sunday? What do you think?

After school Tuesday Jim had some time to kill while Phil was at a meeting. We went to my house for milk and pieces of the last of all the cakes brought to us when we'd moved in. Then we went back to the school yard, where seven guys from our class were shooting baskets. As we approached, the ball rolled toward us. Jim scooped it up and tossed it. It bounced on the rim and then went in. *Wow!*

Someone said, "Teams."

Clive said, "We'll take Jim, and you can have the Gnat and the Brat."

I wanted to sock Clive in his little round mouth; instead, I looked at Jim and shrugged. He answered my shrug with a nod as if to say, *If you're not going to make a fuss, I won't either.*

Jim shot baskets, and Clive guarded me as if I were a threat to their team. He tromped on my toes, elbowed me in the ribs, and kicked me with his knee. When he ran straight into me, I staggered backward and fell. I wasn't hurt and was back on my feet in a minute.

The game ended when Phil came out of the school and called to Jim. It was almost time for *Jack Armstrong* and *Terry and the Pirates* on the radio, but I walked slowly so that Barry could walk with me—if he wanted to. He didn't try to catch up.

Wednesday after school I went back to the school yard. Clive was up to his old tricks, tromping on my toes and elbowing me in the ribs. The ball never came in my direction. I stuck it out that afternoon, but I didn't go back on Thursday.

Friday while we were eating lunch, I asked Jim if he'd go to the picture show with me on Saturday. "*Angels with Dirty Faces,*" I said. "I saw it in Topeka, but I'd sure like to see it again. It's about a gangster and a priest and a bunch of slum kids."

Jim shook his head. Some of the other guys at the table had quit eating and were staring at me.

"We could all go," I said eagerly. "It's a great movie. That James Cagney is—"

Jim put his hand on my arm. "No."

"Do you have something else you have to do on Saturday?"

Jim shook his head again, but another kid spoke up. "Mennonites don't go to movies. The rest of us farm kids come into town when the chores are done and go to the movies on Saturday night."

"You've never been to the picture show, Jim? Any picture show?" That seemed impossible.

"Folks let us see *Goodbye Mr. Chips,*" Jim said.

"Did you like it?" I asked at the same time as another kid muttered that his folks wouldn't let him see any movie.

"Yep." Jim grinned at me, then turned to the boy who had never been to the picture show. "Book was just as good."

When we had finished our lunches, I asked Jim what he did on Saturdays.

"Chores," he answered, then he grinned. "And fishing. Want to go fishing tomorrow?"

I had never been fishing. Actually, I couldn't imagine why anyone would want to spend time sitting beside a muddy creek waiting for a fish to bite at a worm on the end of a string. Still Jim was the only friend I had in Plaintown, and my previous Saturday had been a first-class bore.

"Great!" I hoped I sounded more enthusiastic than I felt.

Early Saturday morning I rode out to Jim's farm on my rusty bike, a hand-me-down from a kid in our Topeka church. Jim introduced me to his dog, Max. Then he told me that the first thing we had to do was dig for worms—slimy, ugly worms. Jim knew where to dig, so it didn't take us as long as I had feared.

Max followed us part of the way into a cornfield and then he lay down with his nose between his paws. Jim went back and scratched the dog's head for a minute.

"Almost as old as I am. Mighty old for a dog," Jim said as we went on through the field and across the corner of a pasture to a slow-moving, dirty creek.

We sat down on the bank, hung worms on the hooks at the end of each of our lines, and dangled our lines in the water. I was using a pole that belonged to Jim's brother who was at college in Newton.

Jim said almost nothing while I babbled about the

weather and school and whatever I could think of. I asked him if he'd always had that crazy eyebrow.

"Nope. Ran into the corner of a table when I was just learning to walk. Bled so much they had to keep it bandaged for a long time. When they took the bandage off, a new look."

"You always look surprised. I like that."

He grinned. After that, nothing, absolutely nothing, happened for what seemed like hours. Mother had made me a lunch. I divided my sandwich with Jim, not because I was hungry but because it was something to do.

When my lunch bag was empty, Jim suggested that we take off our shoes, roll up our pants, and wade to another spot. I would rather have gone home, but the sun was still a long way from the noon-hour position, so I agreed. What else could I do? I couldn't say, *I think I hear my mother calling.* I might have invented a stomachache—if I hadn't just wolfed down half a sandwich. Besides, I asked myself, *What's to do on a Saturday at home?*

We settled ourselves on a bank about fifty feet upstream from where we had been and resumed the long wait. Although there were some clouds in the sky, it was hot, probably in the eighties. I was beginning to feel sleepy. Actually, I was hoping to sleep until it was time to go back to Jim's house.

All of a sudden I felt a tug on my line. At first I thought I had snagged my hook on a rock, but rocks don't flop and tug. I rose to my feet, and Jim told me how to haul the fish in slowly. At last I could see my catch—a catfish, big. I landed it myself!

Only then did I discover that I had tangled my line so that I had to waste minutes before I could try for another fish. In the meantime, Jim caught a perch. I caught a perch, too, and another.

Neither of us caught anything for a while. Then Jim looked up at the sky and said it was time to eat. Max was just where we'd left him. When he saw us he struggled to his feet, wagging his stub of a tail. He licked our hands and walked back to the barnyard with us.

Jim's mother invited me to stay for dinner, served at noon on the farm. Jim and I washed up at the pump outside the kitchen door. I went inside to phone my folks, and then we sat on the back steps to wait for dinner.

Two of Jim's cousins were visiting for the day. They were five-year-old twin boys and they were playing with cars on roads they had made in the dirt. One little boy ran his car into his brother's car, and the wreck was so much fun that they had another and another. That's when I got up and spread my arms, pretending to be an airplane. I zoomed low over the twins' cars and bombed them with a handful of leaves. The twins laughed, and I did it again.

"*BZZZZZZ POW,*" I shouted. "I'm an RAF pilot bombing a German city. I'm paying them back for the London blitz. *BZZZZZZ* . . . ."

"Stop that!" Jim's dad thundered. "We do *not* play war games here!" He turned and strode into the house.

He was angry. I was confused. Jim was embarrassed.

"We're Mennonites," Jim said, as if that explained anything.

I couldn't think what to do except go home. I walked toward my bike at the side of the lane.

"Don't go," Jim pleaded.

"Come to dinner," Jim's dad called from the doorway.

I just stood there for a minute. "I'm sorry," I said to Mr. Reimer, although I didn't know what I had done wrong.

He held out his hand to me. "No, I'm sorry. You didn't know. Come and eat."

The dining room table was three times as big as our dining room table. It had to be big because Jim had a big family. His oldest brother was away at college, but Jim and Phil and their older sister, who had already graduated from high school, and two little sisters, and Jim's parents and grandmother and the hired man ate at that table every day. The grandmother was a very old lady, with more wrinkles than either of my grandmothers. She wore a white cap. Today there were also the twins and me and an old uncle and an aunt, who wore a white cap, and another aunt, who didn't. Fifteen people sitting around one huge table.

In the center of the table were platters heaped high with fried chicken, and the fish we had caught. There was a mountain of mashed potatoes and a bowl the size of a dishpan filled with cabbage slaw and another with vegetables and . . . it went on and on.

But first there was grace. We bowed our heads, and the uncle began to speak. I couldn't understand one word until he said, "Amen." Then Mr. Reimer prayed familiar words about blessing the food to our nourishment.

"German," Jim whispered as he passed me a bowl of beets.

Throughout the meal, the old people chattered in German. The younger Reimers sometimes entered in, and sometimes Jim told me what they were saying: "The flood was pretty bad east of here, but the fields are dry now." That kind of thing. I was too busy eating to pay much attention.

Finally the plates were cleared, and Mrs. Reimer and Jim's older sister brought on apple pies, three of them. It was some meal, let me tell you!

When dinner was over, the little children left the table, and Mrs. Reimer and the younger aunt and the girls rose to wash the dishes.

Jim and I rose, too, but Mr. Reimer motioned for us to sit down again. "I think we should explain our beliefs to Jim's friend, William," he said. "I was surprised to see you entertaining our little ones with pretend bombs, but I am not angry. How were you to know that we Mennonites strongly disapprove of war, all wars, all killing?"

He spoke very softly. Each time I looked up, he was staring directly into my eyes. I kept my head down and folded and refolded my napkin.

Mr. Reimer said that the Methodists and the Mennonites believed many of the same things: God created the world, and Jesus is God's son. They don't baptize babies like we do. Instead, Mennonite children are baptized when they are old enough to choose to be baptized—or not.

"I was baptized when I was twelve," Jim said.

I wanted to ask what would have happened if he'd decided not to be baptized, but I didn't. I was baptized as a baby and confirmed when I was twelve. If I had announced that I didn't want to be confirmed, my dad and mom and the whole Topeka congregation would have fallen apart.

"We have Communion just like you do. We and you try to do good and to follow Christ's teachings," Mr. Reimer said.

"The main difference between us is that we believe that killing people is wrong, however righteous the cause. One of the Commandments is, 'Thou shalt not kill.' You notice that it doesn't say, 'Thou shalt not kill unless the enemy invades your territory or the enemy kills your people.' It says, 'Thou shalt not kill.' Period. Jesus told us to love our enemies and to do good to those who want to hurt us. He said, 'Blessed are the peacemakers.' So we don't fight. Ever. And we don't play at fighting."

I looked up at him then, and he smiled at me. "I just want you to understand. We Kansas Mennonites are going to be tested in the next few years, just as the German and Russian Mennonites are being tested today—and every day. I hope we'll all remain true to what we believe."

The grandmother reached down the table and patted my hand. "Jim's friend. Good boy." She spoke those few words in English.

Phil got up from the table and invited us to shoot baskets. We followed him out to the barn, where a hoop was attached above the door.

When we took a break to get drinks from the pump, I asked a question: "Do you ever fight with one another? I can't fight with my sisters because they are small and girls, but most brothers I know fight sometimes. Do you?"

Jim hung his head. Phil nudged him and said, "Tell your friend the truth."

"Yeah. We shouldn't. But, sometimes . . ."

"Brothers can be so annoying." Phil laughed.

"Do you actually hit one another or do you just fight with your voices?" I asked.

"We wrestle; that's different from fighting," Phil said. "The goal is to prove how strong you are; not to hurt the other guy. When we were little, we sometimes hit to hurt."

"Got punished for it, too," Jim added.

"Do you say things that hurt?"

They looked at one another and grinned sheepishly. At that moment they looked a lot alike, I thought.

"We're supposed to be able to disagree without getting angry," Jim explained.

"Unfortunately, we're not candidates for sainthood." Phil tossed the ball to his brother.

When it was time for the men and boys to start milking, I went into the house to thank Mrs. Reimer for inviting me to dinner. On the table near where Mrs. Reimer was sewing was a kerosene lamp. They had a telephone but no electricity. I wondered why.

The next weekend I cleaned my room on Friday. Saturday morning I rode my bike out to the farm and went fishing with Jim. I came home for lunch. That afternoon we marched at the first game of the football season. Several Saturdays that fall, Jim and I went fishing in the morning and played in the band at football games in the afternoon.

Sunday was the only day of the week when I did not see Jim. Although I still missed my Topeka gang, I had one good friend in Plaintown.

Chapter 4

History was being made daily during that fall of 1941, so we studied the present as well as the past. Our history teacher divided us into three committees to bring in information about the war in Europe, important national news, and state and local news. I thought Jim would want to be on the Europe committee with me, but he refused to even *report* news of the war in Europe. He chose the Kansas committee.

Mary Ellen, one of the girls on our committee who is also a member of our church, brought in a *National Geographic* map of Europe so we could show where the action of the week was taking place. My dad had been given a subscription to *LIFE* magazine, so I brought in pictures showing what mad Hitler was doing to the people of Europe.

My first report was both funny and sad. It was

about an English pilot named Douglas Bader. *LIFE* called him the "spunkiest hero" of the Royal Air Force. He had lost both legs in a flying accident in 1931, but the RAF fixed up a special fighter for him, and he downed at least ten Nazi planes. On August twelfth his plane was set on fire by a *Messerschmitt* over France. He parachuted, breaking one of his artificial legs when he landed behind enemy lines. The Germans told the Red Cross about the broken leg. The RAF had a new leg made for him, attached it to a parachute, and dropped it down to him. We laughed as we imagined that leg floating down to Earth, and then we remembered that this "spunky hero" was a German prisoner.

The United States committee reported on President Roosevelt's order to attack on sight any German or Italian ship in our part of the Atlantic Ocean. They also told about planes and ships that were being built in case we went to war, and about gasoline shortages and price increases.

One member of the Kansas committee kept us up-to-date on how many boys in Plaintown and in Kansas had joined the armed services in the past week. Another member reported on war bond sales.

Every week Jim gave the farm report. Farmers around Plaintown grow winter wheat, so next year's crop had already been planted. It was looking good, Jim said. He compared wheat production of the past summer with the miserable dust bowl years in the 1930s. Clive made a big show of yawning while Jim spoke. I tried to look interested, admiring Jim's eyebrow, if not his boring report.

Homecoming weekend I discovered something else Mennonites cannot do: dance. Jim said that his family thought dancing could lead to sin. I told him that my parents thought dancing was a "social grace." They had made me take ballroom dancing classes while we were living in Topeka. I'd hated it. Only one girl in the class was shorter than me, so I'd had to push these skyscraper girls around the floor while the teacher shouted, "Step two three, step two three."

Before the homecoming dance were the homecoming parade and the homecoming game. The band marched in the parade and played at the game with our arch enemy, Stockport High. At halftime we played "A Pretty Girl Is Like a Melody" as Queen Anne Armstrong and her escort, Phil Reimer, and four other girls and their escorts came onto the center of the field. The mayor put a crown on Anne's head. We won our homecoming game just as Stockport would win theirs a week later.

Clive missed the whole of homecoming because he had the chicken pox. So did Maggie and a lot of children in the elementary school. I don't know why Clive hadn't caught the disease earlier, as Darlene and I and most teenagers had.

Since Clive was home scratching his sores, Barry invited me to go along to the homecoming dance with him and a couple of other guys. We didn't plan to dance; we just wanted to see what was going on—and drink punch and eat cookies.

I watched Anne Armstrong, wondering if she was mad at Phil because he wasn't there. Or was Phil mad at her because she was at the dance without him? The homecoming queen *had* to be there. Besides, she liked to dance. I could see that. When she did the lindy with the captain of the football team, I decided I'd like to be able to do that dance if I could do it with her.

She read my mind! Before the next dance, she came to where I was standing and *she asked me* to dance! She said she'd show me how to lindy, and she did and I did—sort of.

"Now go ask Mary Ellen," Anne whispered as another football player led her back to the dance floor.

When I got to where the guys were standing, they all spoke together one word: "Wow."

I asked Mary Ellen to dance. She wasn't a stranger, and she wasn't any taller than me. We were just beginning to dance pretty well together when the dance ended, so I asked her again. I'd rather have been dancing with Anne.

Monday morning when I left the house, Barry was waiting for me on the front steps.

"I take it your pal Clive is still scratching." I knew I sounded nasty; I felt nasty. Who wants to be the guy on the outside? "I'd have thought you and his other slaves would have skipped school so you could go comfort him in his hour of need."

Barry bounced along beside me, saying nothing.

I broke the silence. "So tell me. What's so great about Clive? Why do you do whatever he tells you to do?"

Barry stopped bouncing, ran his hands through his black curls, and peered into my face. "Are you still mad at Clive? Because he punched you a couple of times?"

"You can call it punching. I call it attacking, beating, thrashing."

Barry hesitated. "Clive was initiating you. That's what he called it: initiation. Afterward, if you—"

"I don't care what he calls it. He beats up on kids smaller than he is. That's bullying. And he looks like a slug and . . ." I walked on.

Barry snatched at my sleeve. "But he's really okay. His uncle is president of the bank, and his father owns the elevator. His grandfather knew Wyatt Earp."

I should explain that the elevator in Plaintown doesn't carry people up and down between floors in a building. It's a group of tall storage towers where farmers bring their wheat to be sold or held for sale. Located just beyond the train station, the Van Dyne elevator looms over the town.

"So how do his rich relatives make Clive a good guy to pal around with?"

Barry bounced even harder. "Clive lives in the biggest house in town, with a rec room in the basement that has a pool table and a Ping-Pong table. They always have lots of Cokes and root beer for us. We go to Clive's on Friday nights."

I hadn't known about those Friday nights. I had to

swallow a couple of times before I could ask another question. "Have you all been initiated the way I was?"

Barry shook his head. "Most of us have been friends since kindergarten. We didn't need to be initiated. We already belonged."

"There must have been other new kids. Did Clive initiate them, too?"

"Yeah. Sort of. But they didn't hold a grudge. We were younger then. Maybe Clive didn't hit as hard." Barry bounced up and down a few times. "Maybe if you'd act like you wanted to be his friend. . . ."

"I have a good friend. His name is Jim Reimer." I was shouting. "He doesn't expect me to beg for the high honor of walking down the street with him or throwing a ball to him in the school yard."

"Jim can't even come to the school yard most afternoons." Barry was shouting, too. "He has to go home and milk the cows, and his friends wear overalls and smell of cow dung and . . ." Barry ran on toward the school.

To my surprise, Barry was waiting to walk home with me at the end of the school day. He ran his hand through his curls and bounced up and down a few times before he spoke. "I know you're mad at Clive—"

"Right. I am mad at him. He calls you *Gnat* and me *Brat,* when he's not calling me *Silly Willy Four-Eyes.* Why don't we call him *Slug?*"

Barry looked at me as if I'd just suggested death by hanging for his buddy Clive. I was about to walk on ahead when he took a deep breath. "While Clive's away, you could start eating lunch with us and you'd be there at the table when he came back and it would be like you'd always been there. You wouldn't have to say or do anything special. You'd just be there. First thing you know, you'd be going to his house on Friday nights with the rest of us, and to the movies on Saturday." He grinned happily. "Good idea?"

"No." I turned away, disgusted.

Chapter 5

It was a crazy fall. It had been mostly warm all through October, and then on the last day of the month we had about a foot of snow—which within days had melted completely. Summer—Indian summer—returned on the weekend of November fifteenth. That was the weekend Jim and I went camping.

Friday after school Phil drove me home to pick up my stuff and then on to the farm where Jim and I strapped our blanket rolls on our backs and picked up our fishing poles and our bags of provisions.

"Hope you remembered matches," Phil called to us as we trudged past the barn. He was holding Max by the collar so the dog wouldn't try to follow us.

Jim looked at me and I looked at Jim and we turned back to the house for a box of matches.

Our destination was a wooded area and stream on

property owned by one of Jim's uncles. We walked through Reimer fields until we came to a narrow dirt road and followed it for more than a mile, passing small farmhouses and big barns until we came to a gate. We climbed over the gate and followed a foot- path. At last we reached a wooded area with trees so tall they blocked most of the last rays of sun. The fallen leaves crackled under our feet. Jim ran ahead. I ran after him, dropping my bag and bedroll where he'd dropped his. Directly ahead was a circle of stones filled with ashes where others had built fires. Beyond was a swift-flowing stream.

Jim put a handful of dry leaves in the center of the fire circle, and we both gathered fallen branches and put them on top of the leaves. While Jim lit the leaves and fanned fire up into the branches, I picked up some larger branches and a few logs that had washed up from the stream. By the time the sky had turned totally dark, our fire was dancing brightly.

Jim pulled a frying pan out of his bag. "So where are those fish we were going to fry for our supper?"

"Right here." I reached into my bag and pulled out two slabs of ham and put them in the frying pan. Jim and I had planned to catch fish for supper; the ham was our backup.

Jim laid two potatoes in the coals. I pulled two oranges out of my bag. He brought a bag of cookies and a bag of dried apples out of his. We each had a tin cup, which we filled with water from the stream. And then we sat side by side on a log near our fire and ate our "fish" supper—all except the potatoes, which would be our before-sleep snack.

"How's it to be a preacher's kid?" he asked me.

I told him about all the moves we'd had to make and about how some people thought the preacher's kids had to be perfect. I told him about Trudy Tarbell and now Mrs. Busybody Van Goose, who were the banes-of-Mom's-existence.

"Clive?"

"He's the bane-of-my existence," I said. Then, suddenly, I laughed. "No, he's not. I don't give a hoot or a holler about him. I've got a good friend." I punched Jim's shoulder. "Tell me about you and your family."

"Been living on the same farm for sixty-five years."

"Before that, your people lived in Germany. Right?"

"Wrong. Two hundred years ago, Catherine the Great invited some of the Mennonite families living in Germany to come to Russia to show the Russian farmers how to be better farmers. She promised them that they would never have to fight in any war. A hundred years later the Czar, who was then in power, told Mennonite leaders that he would no longer honor Catherine's promise. He named a date twenty-five years in the future when Mennonite young men could be called to serve in the Russian army. In the meantime, the Czar would allow them to move to another country if that's what they chose to do."

I laughed and punched Jim again. "That sounds like a paragraph from a history book. Is it?"

He laughed. "Memorized speech. What we say when we're asked where we came from."

"So go on. Tell me more."

"Grossmutter was a little girl at the time, and she and her family and most of their neighbors came to the United States and bought land from the Santa Fe Railroad. The year was 1876. The women had sewed Turkey red wheat into the hems of their dresses. That was the first winter wheat in Kansas. Now most everyone here plants winter wheat."

"So why don't your people speak Russian?"

"Because they never learned Russian in all those years they lived there. They kept to themselves. Problem was they couldn't talk directly to the Czar because none of them knew enough Russian. They had to hire someone to translate, and they couldn't be sure he was saying exactly what they wanted him to say. After that they decided they'd better talk the language of the country where they lived."

"But you know German?"

"Sure. We speak it to our old people and we sing lots of hymns in German and sometimes we pray in German. A problem during the World War. Some people were angry when we wouldn't fight the Germans. *Grossvater* was accused of being a spy, just because he spoke German."

"So what happened to him?"

"Nothing, until he refused to buy war bonds. Then men came out to our farm in the middle of the night and dragged him out of bed. They smeared tar all over his body and sprinkled feathers over the tar." Jim flapped his elbows and cackled like a chicken, exactly like a chicken. "That's what they did."

"So did he buy bonds then?"

By the light of the fire I watched Jim bow his head and bite his lip. "You don't have to tell me," I said. Then I laughed. "The radio sound effects people should know about you—in case they ever need chicken cackles."

He smiled for just a moment. Then he turned serious again. "Friends tell friends things, so I'll tell you the truth. When my grandfather died, *Grossmutter* found five bonds that he'd bought. She was so ashamed, she wanted to burn them, but my dad said that the Lord would show us what to do with them."

"And did He?"

"We think so. During the drought and dust storms, our neighbor couldn't make his mortgage payments. Dad gave our neighbor the bonds. He wasn't a Mennonite, you see."

I didn't see, but I didn't ask. *Friends tell friends things*— but they don't have to tell them everything. Besides, I'd already heard more words from Jim that night beside our campfire than I'd heard in the entire time I'd known him.

We spread our bedrolls near the fire and sat on them while we ate our potatoes. I hadn't known that potatoes without butter or gravy or even salt could be delicious. The moon was bright and the stars twinkled and I had a good friend beside me. All felt right with the world.

• • •

We woke with the sun. We had slept in our clothes, so we didn't have to waste time dressing. The night before, while I was gathering wood, I'd found a good place to find worms. While I dug the worms, Jim built a new fire. It was so cold, I wrapped myself in one of my blankets before I went down to the stream.

"Red blanket'll frighten the fish away," Jim said as he adjusted his gray blanket around his shoulders. He was wrong. That red blanket, or something else—maybe hunger—drove the fish right onto our hooks.

I never had such a good breakfast in my whole life as those fish we caught and fried ourselves.

By the time we were ready to close up our camp, the sun was high overhead and the earth was warm. We doused our fire and packed up our gear and started back.

We were swinging down the center of the dirt road, between a pasture and a wheat field, when we heard a woman screaming. The only word I could make out was "no."

Surprised, I turned to question Jim, but he had dropped his gear in the middle of the road and was unstrapping his bedroll. Within seconds he was running toward the pasture.

"Red blanket," Jim shouted.

I didn't stop to ask why. I just pulled my blanket from my bedroll and ran after Jim. As soon as I reached the fence, I saw a bull—and a baby. The barbed-wire fence beside the road turned a corner away from the road. Back about the length of a football field from the road, the baby had crawled under the fence and was toddling into the pasture. The bull lowered his head. His horns were enormous. He was plodding slowly toward the child. Jim was running, full speed, on a diagonal across the field toward the child. The mother, who looked like she was going to have another baby very soon, stood by the fence calling to the child.

I'd read about bullfights, so I knew what Jim wanted me to do. While he ran toward the child, I crawled under the fence and started waving my blanket. The bull ignored me. I shouted. If there are special words you are supposed to say to bulls, I don't know them, so I just made all the noise I could.

The bull began to trot—straight toward the child. I ran into the pasture, screaming and waving the blanket in a wide arc. When the bull was about ten feet from the child, Jim ran right in front of him and scooped up the child. Jim ran toward the fence. The bull was right behind. I ran toward the bull, shouting and waving the blanket, but it was as if I weren't there.

Jim moved the child from his hip and thrust her forward across the fence into the mother's outstretched hands. Then he dropped to the ground and rolled under the fence. His jacket caught on the barbed wire, but Jim rolled right out of his jacket as the bull crashed into the fence and roared as he hit the wire.

Then he turned toward me and my red blanket. I crushed the blanket into a tight ball and ran back toward the road. When I had crawled under the fence, I looked back at the bull, who was still half a football field away from me.

I walked along the road to the corner of the fence and then along the fence to where Jim was sitting in the grass, sweat pouring down his face, his shoulders heaving. I flopped down beside him, and the little girl began to climb over both us, laughing and cooing. She didn't know she'd just missed being gored to death. Her mother brought us a dipper of water. She was crying as she began patting Jim on the shoulder and saying "thank you, thank you" over and over. Jim took a deep breath and grinned at me.

I couldn't think of a thing to say, but I knew I'd never forget the moment when Jim ran right in front of the bull and snatched up the little girl and turned his back on the bull and ran toward the fence.

"You are one brave kid!" I said, at last.

"So are you."

I shook my head. "Not I. I was under the fence before the bull came anywhere near me."

"Good. Can't think why you'd want to stick around to chat with that bull."

"That's what I should have done. I could have told him he was a big, bad bully to frighten that little girl's mommy."

"And me. That big, bad bull scared me. That's for sure." We laughed together. That's another thing good friends do.

We were still laughing when a truck drove into the yard. The stuff we'd dropped on the road was in it.

"Want a ride?" the driver called. We climbed into the cab, and Jim introduced me to the driver, whose last name was also Reimer.

By the time Phil drove me home, my folks had already heard from the mother of the little girl. My mother made a big fuss.

"Glad it turned out okay," my dad said. "How was the camping and the fishing?"

I told them about the potato cooked in the coals and the fish we'd had for breakfast. I told them that Jim and I were planning lots of camping trips for the spring and summer. Maybe we'd even set out on our bikes and be gone for a whole week.

When I went to bed that night, I lived over every minute from when we set out from Jim's house on Friday night until I got home. What a great time!

One night during the next week, while Mom and I were doing the dishes, she asked me how I was liking Plaintown.

"It's okay," I said. I couldn't tell Mom how Clive and the town kids from my class met on Friday nights. She'd likely complain to one of the mothers, and then I really would be the guy everyone loved to hate. "Jim is a good friend," I said. "And school is okay. I like my history class. And band. And English. And . . ."

"Sounds like high school is terrific." Mom sighed deeply. "Everyone in this family is happy. Maggie is learning to read. That's what's important to her. Darlene is surrounded by new friends and their games. You seem to be comfortable. Dad has more people to preach to than ever before—and more people to help."

"What about you?" I asked. "You like it here?"

She nodded her head, and then slowly the nod became a shake. "Truth? I might if I didn't have to put up with all the kind suggestions of people like Mrs. Van Dyne. She thinks that Maggie should behave in a more ladylike manner. And she thinks I should serve cream cheese and olive sandwiches to the church women when they meet here—not at the church but in the parsonage—next week, so everyone can check up on my housekeeping." Mom dropped the dishrag and ran out of the kitchen.

I finished drying the dishes and then I emptied the dishpan and scrubbed the sink. I felt sorry for Mom—and for me. Like it or not, we were stuck here with the Van Dynes. I'd complained about moving so much that Mom had asked Dad to ask the bishop to keep us here until I was graduated from high school, and the bishop had agreed. Maybe we could get the Van Dynes to move. Fat chance! Besides, I'd hate to move away from Jim—unless I could move back to Jack and George and Pinky and Pete.

When she came to say good night, Mom sat down on the bed beside me and stroked my hair back from my forehead. "About this evening," she whispered. "I'm sorry. I should not have talked like that. I know I'm going to like it here." She stopped. "I love your dad so much that I want to be a good minister's wife. I really do. The job just doesn't come naturally to me. But I'm trying."

"That's all we expect of you," I said, using the exact same words and the exact same tone she and Dad use when I complain that something is hard but that I'm trying.

Mom and I laughed together. I wonder if Dad understood how hard Mom tried. Or did he just assume that witnessing for the Lord is as inspiring for us as it is for him?

Chapter 6

President Roosevelt said that December 7, 1941, was ". . . a date which will live in infamy."

That Sunday began as a special day for me. It was so warm that I didn't plan to wear my heavy jacket. Mom and I were about to argue about that when she gasped and pointed to my socks. Inches of ankle showed beneath my suit pants. Inches of wrist showed beneath my sleeves. The suit I had worn on our first Sunday in Plaintown three months earlier was definitely too small.

When we went up to the sanctuary after Sunday school, I measured myself beside Barry. My shoulder was at least two inches above his. That morning I knew for sure that I was emerging from shrimphood.

On Sundays, we always eat our main meal around one in the afternoon. After our roast beef and spice cake dinner on that special Sunday, I helped with the dishes. When I stretched out on the rug in the living room to read the funnies, Darlene complained that I took up too much space. That was such a beautiful complaint that I grinned instead of answering back.

I was truly happy that afternoon until about three o'clock, when I scooted over to the radio and switched it on: BOMBS ON PEARL HARBOR!

Even as I was calling my folks to come listen, I was thinking that it couldn't be true.

"It's a fake," I announced as soon as Mom and Dad were standing in the archway between the living and dining rooms. "Like that radio program that had people thinking the Martians had landed in New Jersey. It's just like that. Isn't it?"

Neither of my parents answered. They just stood there, staring at one another and listening to the radio announcer, who said that the Japanese had attacked Pearl Harbor and nearby airfields at 7:55 A.M., Honolulu time, which was 12:55 Kansas time.

Members of our congregation began calling, one after another. Our phone is on the wall in the hall behind the stairs, over a high shelf with a pad of paper for messages. After the first hour, Mom sent me to the basement for the stepladder. Dad sat on that ladder and talked on the phone all afternoon, except for the times when Mom relieved him.

"Yes, I believe it to be true, Mrs. Stevens. . . . Come to the church at seven-thirty tonight for a prayer vigil."

"Yes, Ernie, I know you served in the last war. How

old were you then? And now? You'll be needed here, Ernie. Come to the church at seven-thirty. We'll need you to comfort the others. No, perhaps it would be better if you didn't tell them about the trenches and the blood. . . ."

"Bobby can't sign up tonight, Mrs. Bart. The recruitment office is surely closed. You're his mother. Convince him to wait until tomorrow. See if you can get him to come with you to the church."

When Mom was on the phone, she suggested that someone call Marian, the church organist. "We'll want to sing. No, definitely not 'Onward Christian Soldiers' or 'God of Our Fathers' either." Mom sounded frantic. Then she lowered her voice and spoke very slowly. "Quiet, soothing hymns. 'Sweet Hour of Prayer' or 'Nearer My God to Thee,' No, they don't have anything to do with war. That's the point. We must stay calm."

At youth group we were supposed to be working on our service project, cutting holly leaves out of green construction paper to tie to the candy canes we would distribute when we went to sing carols at the old people's home. Not a single leaf was cut. The adult leaders suggested that we practice singing carols. We didn't do that either. We just talked about what we were going to do to show those dirty Japs a thing or two. Several of the kids had brothers who were already in the army or in the Kansas guard.

One of these was Clive, who stood up and puffed out his chest and bragged about his brother. "Chester could have gone to Princeton–that's the best college in the country—but instead he joined the Army Air Force. He's just about finished flight school. My brother is prepared to defend his country."

I was flabbergasted. No one had told me that Clive had a brother. I was also impressed. I didn't care about Clive's pool table or his uncle's bank or his father's elevator, but to have a brother who was in flight school—that was worth bragging about!

One of the seniors in our group would be eighteen in February. He had been planning to go to K. State. The draft age was twenty-one, but he said he wasn't going to wait to be drafted, or even to graduate from high school. He planned to enlist as soon as he'd blown out the candles on his birthday cake.

Usually evening church is a lot like a revival meeting. Dad prays and tells a story from the Bible, but mostly we sing—foot-tapping gospel songs like "O How I Love Jesus" or "Standing on the Promises of God."

My sisters seldom went to evening church, but this Sunday was different. Dad said that in a time of crisis, the church was the place to be and we would all five attend the service. When I went up to the sanctuary, I knew immediately that it was going to be a quiet service. Only a few lights had been turned on, so the church was dim. The organist was playing soft hymns, going from one to the next. Anne Armstrong sat beside the organist and sang "Make Me a Blessing." Dad read the twenty-third Psalm: "The Lord is my shepherd; I shall not want . . ." It was like a funeral; people were crying.

• • •

School the next day was something else! The principal was at the door as we entered the building. He directed band members to the band room, glee club members to the music room, and everyone else to the auditorium. We picked up our instruments and took our places on the stage where we played "The Star-Spangled Banner" better than ever before. Those who were not in the band sang with fervor, as if phrases like "What so proudly we hailed" had new meaning. The glee club sang the song that begins, "Breathes there a man with soul so dead who never to himself has said, 'This is my own, my native land . . .'"

The principal announced a new Patriots Club. We'd practice marching and we'd collect scrap metal and tinfoil. "We'll do whatever we can to support our brave men in uniform. If we can count on you to do your part in bringing a speedy peace to our land, stand up. Stand up for the good old U. S. of A. and our brave soldiers and sailors and marines."

Everybody stood and cheered. I *thought* it was everybody until I looked down and saw Phil Reimer, the president of the student body and the captain of the basketball team, *sitting* in the front row with his hands clasped together in his lap and his head bowed! Anne Armstrong stood looking down at him and shaking her head.

I spun around to look at Jim just as he dropped back into his seat. He must have started to stand with the rest of us and then changed his mind. While I watched, he leaned forward with his arms resting on his knees and his head bowed low over the trumpet he held in his hands.

The Reimers weren't the only ones sitting. There were several members of the band and the chorus and more than a dozen others facing us from their seats in the auditorium. *How could they just sit there when every person was needed to win the war?* I had heard what Jim's father had said about Mennonites hating war, but that was before the Japs attacked us. Everything was different now.

If I were taller—and if I had begun to shave—I'd have been over at the recruiting office right that minute. I'd have lied about my age. I had read about a boy only fourteen years old who had joined the Royal Air Force. No one knew he had lied until he was dead, shot down. He must have had a beard. Every morning I rubbed my upper lip, hoping that the few hairs I had cut with scissors the week before had suddenly become a thick growth that could be removed only with lots of white lather and a sharp razor.

That day we marched between classes singing "Anchors Away," and "Over Hill Over Dale," and "From the Halls of Montezuma," and my favorite, the air force song, "Off We Go into the Wild Blue Yonder."

At lunchtime I joined Jim at our regular table, but I didn't say anything, waiting for him to tell me what was going on. He'd said it: *Friends tell friends things.* When I finished my sandwich, he handed me a cookie from his lunch but he still remained silent.

"So why didn't you stand up?" I heard the impatience in my voice.

Everyone at the table seemed to freeze, some with their sandwiches halfway to their mouths. Only their eyes moved—from me to Jim and back to me.

"I'm a Mennonite." Jim spoke softly, calmly. "You know that."

"So?"

"We don't support wars. You know that, too." His voice was becoming harsh.

"So?"

"So we will not participate in Mr. Roosevelt's war." Jim, the peace lover, was angry. I fancied I could see smoke billowing from his nostrils.

I was angry, too; fuming, to be exact. "'Mr. Roosevelt's war'? I'd say it was America's war. You want the Japs to come right on across the Pacific and bomb California? You want the Nazis to come right across the Atlantic and bomb New York and Washington, D.C.? Is that what you want?"

"I don't want anyone to fight. Period." Jim was shouting.

"American ships and planes have been destroyed. Americans have died. So what do you think we should do? Send someone to tell Hitler and Hirohito that they are naughty boys? Do you think that if we ask nicely, they'll pick up their nasty toys and go home?"

When Jim didn't respond, I clenched my fists. I wanted to sock him hard, right under his stubborn chin. Instead, I got up from the table, climbed over the bench, and marched to the middle of the lunchroom. *Where to?* I looked at Barry. When our eyes met, he turned to look at Clive. *Did Clive own that whole darn table?* I'd finished my lunch, so I jammed the rest of Jim's cookie into my mouth and walked out of the lunchroom.

I spent the rest of the lunch hour in the library, wondering if I'd be spending every lunch hour from that time on in the library. The alternative was to beg Clive for the privilege of sitting at the same table with him. *Why would I do that? Clive didn't own the table.*

By the next day, the lines were drawn. When I entered the lunchroom, I saw that all the Mennonites from all the classes were sitting together at two tables in the far corner. Anne Armstrong, who usually ate with Phil, sat with the other cheerleaders.

Jim looked up and saw me standing in the doorway, but he didn't grin. He didn't even nod. He just lowered his eyes and unwrapped his sandwich. That was okay with me; I wouldn't have gone near that gang of do-nothings if Jim had begged me.

My shoulders felt almost too heavy to shrug, but I shrugged them anyway. At almost the same moment, my eyes met Allen's. He scooted down the bench to make room for me at one end of a freshmen boys table; Clive was at the other end. When I had finished my lunch, I counted the kids at the two tables in the corner and concluded that there were twenty-two Mennonites—plus any who might have been out sick— out of a total enrollment of about one hundred ninety.

"Hey, Silly Willy," Clive called. "Why aren't you sitting with your German-speaking Nazi pals? I thought you liked those yellow-bellied traitors. Did you decide to be a true-blue American after all?"

"You got one thing right, Clive," I shouted back. "I am a true-blue loyal American."

Clive didn't respond.

At the first Patriots meeting, we set up a sky-watch committee. A senior passed around pictures of American planes. I could identify every one of them, so he made me the chairman of the freshmen division. My job was to keep my eyes on the sky. If a plane flew over that I couldn't identify, I would call a number he would give me to alert the authorities. Kansas was right in the center of the country; we could be attacked by either the Germans beyond the Atlantic Ocean or the Japs beyond the Pacific Ocean.

That's what we thought until Allen laughed. "There isn't a plane in the world that could fly all the way from Japan to Kansas and back to Japan," he said. "Not even from Germany and back to Germany."

"Ever hear of an aircraft carrier, Mr. Wise Guy," Clive said, sneering.

For the first time in my life, I felt like clapping for Clive. An aircraft carrier could sneak up near California or New York or Florida or Texas and send off a whole squadron of planes aimed right at Kansas, the heart of America.

That night, as soon as Dad finished saying grace, I announced that I was chairman of the freshmen division of the E.P.S, enemy plane spotters.

I didn't expect my know-nothing sisters to be impressed—but my parents?

"Really?" Mom said, which is what she would have said if I'd announced that I'd sharpened a pencil. Then she turned to Maggie. "Just one piece of cauliflower, darling."

"I'll be busy morning, noon, and night," I announced.

"What will you be doing at night?" Dad asked. "Besides sleeping?"

"I'll be at my window, watching," I said

"And how will you identify the planes at night?"

I hadn't thought of that.

"Look, William," Dad said in his oh-so-patient voice that meant I was in for a long lecture. "Let's get things into perspective here. War is not fun and games. Bombs, like rain, fall on the just and on the unjust." The "rain on the just and the unjust" was from the Bible, of course.

Dad continued his mini-sermon: "Innocent people get killed in war, and in the end, no one really wins."

"You think we should all be Mennonites and sit back and invite the Japs and the Germans to take over our country?" I asked.

He shook his head sadly. "No. Americans will have to fight. Now. But one day the people of the world will 'beat their swords into plowshares and their spears into pruning hooks; nation shall not lift up sword against nation, neither shall they learn war any more.'"

More Bible verses! I lowered my eyes and stabbed my pork chop with my fork.

When Darlene and I had cleared the dinner plates and brought on the cookies and canned peaches, Dad spoke again. "Let me tell you my news. Reverend Bob Cole came by today. He's young, no family, and eager to serve as a chaplain. If the army takes him, I'll serve his church as well as my own. The bishop has agreed."

"But Bob's church is twenty miles away." Mom sounded really concerned about what Dad had to say.

"Yes. It's too far for his congregation to come here. They'll have to have their church service before or after ours. One thing, it'll keep my sermons short." He laughed.

"There's more to ministering than preaching." Mom bit her lip, which is what she does when she's worried. "What about visiting the sick and presiding at funerals and weddings? What about counseling? Think how everyone called you on Sunday. Another church will mean that many more people will be depending on you."

"I know. It will be more work, but I'll be making it possible for one chaplain to comfort young men on the battlefield."

That was the first wartime change in our family. It meant more work for Dad and more money for us—even though the bane-of-Mom's-existence tried to get the congregation to reduce Dad's salary by the amount he would be receiving from Bob Cole's congregation.

Incidentally, Mrs. Busybody Van Goose had not done anything about the ugly couch.

Although I checked the sky every night before I went to sleep, and several times during the day, I never spotted an enemy plane—and I never received a number to call if I did spot one. That project fizzled before it ever began. No one really expected an enemy plane to make it to Kansas.

Chapter 7

Christmas and war were all mixed up together that year. When I was little, I loved the pageant and the huge tree in the corner of the sanctuary and the boxes of hard candy we all received. Now that I was practically an adult, I asked to be excused. My request was denied, and on the Sunday afternoon before Christmas I was marching down the side aisle in an old choir robe with a striped scarf hanging from my shoulders and a cardboard crown on my head while everyone sang "We Three Kings."

Christmas Eve was three nights later. There were *two* memorable things about the Christmas Eve service. One was Anne Armstrong singing "O Holy Night." The other was Clive's brother, Chester, who came to church in uniform. He was taller than Clive and slimmer, blond but not as nearly white as Clive. His eyes were larger and brighter blue. In short, Chester was much better looking than his brother.

Clive stuck to him like adhesive tape as they walked toward the doors at the end of the service. When they reached the vestibule, Chester whispered something to Clive and then took Anne's arm and led her out to his car. Clive stood on the church steps watching them until the car had turned the corner. In the meantime, I struggled with the Tenth Commandment. I did not covet Clive's house, or his ox, or his ass. But his brother? I couldn't help coveting Clive's brother.

Later I also coveted his bike, a fantastic black and silver pair of wheels that had been in the window at Schultz's hardware store. I had spent a lot of time before Christmas gawking at that bike and picturing myself speeding through town on it. I knew it would not be under our tree on Christmas morning; it cost too much. Still, I couldn't help hoping—and praying—and hinting.

I received underwear, a sweater, a huge map of the world, and a great model plane kit.

On Monday, December twenty-ninth, sixteen of Plaintown's "finest young men" were scheduled to board the train that would take them to Fort Riley and Fort Leavenworth. Volunteers and draftees expected to be inducted, and the seasoned soldiers expected to be sent to fight in the Pacific.

"I object to calling boys who have been in the army

for a few weeks, at most a few months, 'seasoned,'" Mom declared.

"What do you need except a little salt and pepper to season a soldier?" I laughed at my own joke.

Mom did not laugh. She reminded me that we were talking about human beings, in which case "seasoned" meant experienced or well-trained. I knew that.

Dad objected to calling them "boys." "They may not be old enough to vote, but they are old enough to die for their country. Therefore, they are men." Incidentally, the draft age had already been lowered to twenty.

With almost no time to prepare, the town sent its poorly seasoned young men off in style. Everyone who had ever played in the high school band was invited to bring an instrument to the train station. We needed some of those old folks because the seven Mennonites in the band stayed home. I hadn't expected Jim to come, so why was I disappointed?

We played marches while a crowd assembled on the platform. Veterans of the last war were selling American flags for a dime each. The mayor shouted into a megaphone—about our brave young men and the evil enemy—on and on.

When, at last, we heard the train whistle, Dad climbed up on a baggage cart and raised his arms out over the crowd. "'The Lord bless thee, and keep thee,'" he prayed. "'The Lord make His face shine upon thee, and be gracious unto thee: The Lord lift up His countenance upon thee,' and bring peace to the world." My father's response to the war had been disappointingly cool, but his prayer, from the Old Testament, seemed just right.

We played "America the Beautiful" as the train chugged into the station and "The Washington Post March" as it pulled out. When the last car of the train was out of sight, the crowd surged into the street in front of the station and then turned south onto Main Street. We were all marching to the beat of one bass drum; many were waving flags.

Suddenly a man's voice soared out over the crowd. "Shun Schultz." He shouted it again, and others joined in. It became a chant. "Shun Schultz," drumbeat, "Shun Schultz . . ."

Clive rode up beside me on his beautiful black and silver bike. "Schultz is a yellow-bellied Mennonite," he shouted. "Mrs. Schultz came here straight from Germany. She can't even speak good English. Shun Schultz." Clive rode off on the bike his folks had bought from Mr. Schultz.

The "Shun Schultz" chant continued as the people in the front of the crowd marched up onto the sidewalk. A stepladder was standing on the sidewalk next to the door of the hardware store. On the top of the ladder was a sign that said 50% OFF. Tools were displayed on the steps. Several men grabbed tools and lifted them high overhead.

A hammer flew through the air. The sound of shattering glass silenced the chanting crowd—for an instant–until someone shouted, "Shun Schultz," again, and others resumed the chant. I stood in stunned silence while the sheriff and a couple of deputies and my father and the mayor pushed through the crowd.

"Head on home, now," the mayor shouted. "Don't tarnish this proud day. Head on home."

As the crowd began to disperse, Barry ran along beside me chattering like a squirrel. "I wonder who threw that hammer. Wish I'd done it. Schultz and his wife are spies."

"Shut up, Barry!" I hissed.

He stopped and stared at me. "What's the matter with you? You think it's okay for those Mennonite guys to let their pals do all the fighting?"

I shrugged my shoulders.

Barry shrugged his shoulders, too. "I was going to invite you to go with me to Clive's rec room. Clive said we should come by after lunch. But I guess you wouldn't be interested. Expect your idea of a good time is cleaning out barns and milking cows." He ran on ahead.

I walked home slowly and stretched out on my bed to stare at the cracks in my ceiling. I didn't know any of the boys/men who were going off to war. Most of them wanted to go. *Join the Navy and see the world* and all that. I would want to go. Yet some of the young men would never come home. That's what happened in war. People died.

Hitler had already killed thousands of people. He had to be stopped! Hirohito had killed thousands of

Chinese, and now he was sending his planes to bomb Americans. *He* had to be stopped! There was no alternative. That's what *I* thought.

The Mennonites thought differently. But why should a crowd of people turn against one Mennonite? Did anyone know how Mr. Schultz felt in his heart? Maybe he thought his church took this pacifism thing too far.

And Jim? Maybe he understood the need for Americans to do everything they could to win this war. Maybe he was just pretending to go along with his family and his church. One day, I'd ask him. *Friends tell friends things.*

With my mind still in a muddle, I went downstairs for lunch.

"I don't know why either," Mom said, even though I had not asked the question aloud.

That afternoon I took a stack of old *LIFE* magazines to my room. I cut out a picture for Maggie. It was a photograph of the first baby rhinoceros born in a zoo, the Brookfield Zoo in Chicago. It weighed more at birth than Maggie weighed now.

Before Pearl Harbor, I'd begun to cover some of the roses on my dirty tan wallpaper with pictures of planes. I cut out and pasted up more that afternoon. One showed squadrons of training planes flying over the mountains of California before being delivered to army and navy bases. Another was of substratosphere parachutists who fell for twenty-nine thousand feet before they opened their chutes for the last fifteen hundred feet. There was a picture of the world's biggest war plane, a B-19. And a picture of two P-40s that had been shattered by bombs at Pearl Harbor.

Mom and I had taped the huge map I got for Christmas to the wall above my desk. That afternoon I read about the panzer attacks in Africa, and I marked the places on my map. I also marked the places where Americans had been fighting in the Pacific.

One picture I folded and put in my pocket. After we had said grace and Dad had served our dinner plates, I turned to Mom. "Do you think Mrs. Cornelius Vanderbilt is a fine lady? Do you think she has good table manners?"

"I know nothing about Mrs. Cornelius Vanderbilt except that she has a lot of money. I assume she has good table manners." Mom laughed. "Has she invited you for a visit?"

"Not yet. Do you think her guests have good table manners?"

"I assume they do. You'd better be practicing yours—so you'll behave appropriately. I'd be humiliated if my son used the wrong fork."

"Never fear," I said, pulling the page from *LIFE* out of my pocket and spreading it out in the center of the table. "I'll fit in just fine," I told her. "See this man. He has his elbows on the table. And look at these people. They're eating even though these people over here haven't been served yet. What do you think of that?"

Mom laughed again. "Maybe when forty-six people are all sitting at one table, they aren't expected to wait for everyone to be served."

Dad chuckled and shook his finger at me. "Remember this: You can behave any way you like when you are at Mrs. Vanderbilt's house; at Mrs. Spencer's home, we do not put our elbows on the table and we do wait until everyone has been served." Dad grinned. "You ask me if I want to eat at Mrs. Vanderbilt's house, and I'll tell you that I'd rather eat the food Mrs. Spencer prepares—with love—than all the snails and caviar in Mrs. Vanderbilt's mansion." He threw a kiss across the table to Mom.

That made be feel good for the first time since the train had tooted out of the station.

The second week of the Christmas vacation was the loneliest week of my life. I wrote a long letter to Jack and George and Pinky and Pete. I told them that one of the cheerleaders had taught me to lindy. I described the camping trip and how I had waved a red blanket to distract the bull while my friend saved the life of a little child. I told them about the Patriots Club. My letter was a masterpiece of deception. My old buddies would never guess that I no longer had anyone to pal around with.

I had plenty of time that week to build the plane from the kit I had received for Christmas and to read to Maggie. My dad, who seldom had time for games, played checkers with me almost every night that week.

Did he know that I had no friends? I doubt it. My dad wanted us to eat good food, go to bed early, be polite, behave ourselves, trust in the Lord, pay attention in school and Sunday school, and "love one another." He didn't care about our friends.

Chapter 8

When school started again on the first Monday of the new year, our homeroom teacher announced that we were to collect scrap metal and newspapers, which we'd bring to a fenced-in area of the school yard as soon as the weather warmed and the snow was gone.

"We must all do everything we can to contribute to the war effort," she said. "We must save fat and cans. We must buy defense stamps."

We'd already been buying defense stamps every Thursday at school, but she urged us to buy more.

"I know we can depend on most of you to do your best for the war effort. I hope that even you, Dorothy, and you, Sylvia, will do you part. Will you?"

While the teacher waited for an answer, we all turned to stare at the two Mennonite girls who sat near the back of the room.

"Will you?" the teacher repeated.

Dorothy took a deep breath and stood beside her desk. "No, ma'am, we will not."

She and the teacher stared at one another for a minute that seemed like an hour. I'd have babbled on and on, one excuse after the other, but Dorothy just stood there and said nothing.

"You may sit down, Dorothy, but I hope you and Sylvia will both tell your parents that it will be difficult for you if you do not cooperate in these all-school war efforts."

After class I saw Mary Ellen talking with the Mennonite girls. I wondered what she could find to say to them.

When we entered our history class early and together, I had a chance to ask her. "I wanted to talk with them, but I couldn't think of anything to say. Did you tell them you thought the teacher was unfair?"

Mary Ellen shook her head. "No, I told them I admired them for standing up for what they thought was right."

"Do *you* think the Mennonites are right?"

"No, but I wish they were. You couldn't have a war if nobody was willing to fight."

"Emphasize *nobody*. You can't let fighters take over whole countries because no one will oppose them."

"You're right. But, still, I think it may be more courageous not to fight in this case than to fight."

"Right," I said. "Thanks for talking to them."

"You wish you could talk to Jim. Don't you, William?"

I shrugged, and we went to our desks.

It snowed on and off all that week. Saturday morning I took my rusty old sled to the only hill in town. Most of the guys in our class were there. Clive, who had a Flexible Flyer, of course, didn't bother me that day; he just ignored me. Allen also had a Flexible Flyer, and he let me take it down the slope four times. It went twice as fast as my rusty old hunk-of-junk. I was mighty tired of making do with hand-me-downs. The only new items I seemed to get were socks and underwear.

During our last climb back up the hill, Allen said he was hoping to make the junior varsity basketball team. He had practiced almost every weekday over the holidays and every afternoon after school.

"That's great. I'll hope for you, too," I said. "Did Jim come out to practice with you guys?"

Allen shook his head.

"But Phil was there?"

Allen nodded. He looked both puzzled and sad. "Must be hard to be them and have to pretend there isn't a war on," he said.

I nodded and didn't say anything for a while, and then I decided to share an idea I'd had with Allen. "It'd be especially hard if they don't agree that all war is wrong. What if they really want to stand up and sing with us? Maybe Jim begged his folks to let him come play his trumpet at the train station."

"Never thought of that. Maybe they have to go along with their folks' religion, just like you'd have to be a Methodist whether you agreed with your dad or not."

"And you? Could you decide to go to another church or no church?"

"Yep. If I told my folks I wanted to take a vacation from church, they'd say, 'Go ahead.' I was thinking of doing that, but then you moved to town."

Did Allen say that he came to church because of me? I couldn't believe that, but I knew I was grinning when we reached the top of the hill. Allen took his last run on his Flexible Flyer. I followed on my rusty tub. When he reached the bottom, he waited for me. "Want to come to the Roxy this afternoon, William? I'll meet you outside."

After lunch as I ran toward the Roxy, I saw Allen, his red hair shining like a new penny. A bunch of guys from our class were standing with him. We all went in together and sat in the same row, Clive at one end, and Allen and me at the other. That was that. From then on, I went to the picture show almost every Saturday afternoon.

The first history report I gave in the new year came from the January fifth *LIFE*. The article said that the war in the Far East hinged on Manila and Singapore. I passed around a map showing where the

Japs had landed in the Philippines and in the Indian Ocean. The January nineteenth *LIFE* announced that after forty years the U.S. had temporarily lost control of the Philippines. A month later the Japanese had taken Singapore.

The war news was bad, but every week I was covering more and more of the roses on my bedroom walls with pictures of American planes. The February second issue of *LIFE* had eight pages of U.S. war planes. Of course we would win the war, just as soon as we had enough of those planes. Some people had already left Plaintown to work in the big aircraft factory in Wichita.

One night I asked Dad if he'd thought about working in the Wichita plant. "The workers are making lots of money, and since you have a college degree, they'd make you a boss." What I didn't say aloud was that if he were working in a factory, I would no longer be a preacher's brat, and Mom could have a house of her own.

Dad looked at me as if I'd suggested that we move to the South Pole. "And leave my congregation, both of my congregations? Bob is doing his part by ministering to our servicemen; I'm doing my part by filling his shoes—trying to fill his shoes—here in Kansas. I prize my 'high calling of God in Jesus Christ.' Both congregations need me."

My dad thought that people couldn't do anything important without him. He was there when they were sick or dying or marrying. He baptized babies

and confirmed older children. If people couldn't figure out what to do about anything, they'd ask Dad.

Mom sometimes laughed at the problems they
wanted him to solve. "It won't be long now until
they're asking you how much salt to put in the stew,"
she'd say.

But the war did change life at our house. Just one
week after I'd suggested that Dad get a job at an aircraft factory, Mom made a truly wacky announcement.
The man who was the principal of the elementary
school and a member of our church asked her to teach
fourth grade. The present teacher was leaving to marry
a soldier who was stationed in California.

I couldn't believe anyone would expect Mom to
work for money. She had enough to do at home and at
the church. The only women I knew who worked had
no husbands, or their husbands had no jobs. Female
schoolteachers were either very young or old maids. I
remembered how Mom had hidden on that first day in
Plaintown and I knew she could never go "out" to
work.

"Of course, you won't do it," I said, hoping that she
didn't feel too bad about the money she couldn't earn.

"You wouldn't teach my class," Darlene wailed.
"I'd be so embarrassed."

"I thought you were in fifth grade, Darlene. Didn't
you hear me say I was going to teach fourth grade?"

"You're going to accept the job?" I couldn't believe
what I was hearing. "What about Maggie?"

"What about Maggie? She's in school all day. We'll

come home together, Maggie and I, and Darlene, if she can bear to be seen with her working mother." The tone of her voice and the flash of her eyes said, *Careful there.*

Nevertheless, I couldn't help asking one more question. "What about all the things you do for the church?"

"Someone else will have to arrange the church suppers and prepare the devotions and bake the cookies for the women's meetings. Barry's mother is going to teach my Sunday school class for the first month or two, until I get organized. If your father needs me for anything special, I'll be there. Other people will have to get along without me."

She sighed deeply, and I saw that her hands were trembling. "Don't you think I can manage a group of nine-year-olds, William? I taught while Dad was at seminary. I was a good teacher then, and I'll be a good teacher now."

Dad came around the table and began to rub her shoulders. "Mom's working means that we'll all have to chip in. Don't any of you plan anything for Saturday mornings. That's when we're all going to clean house while Mom does the wash. No one will leave until the house sparkles."

Darlene and I groaned.

"Enough," Dad said sharply. "If you can't see yourselves helping for the pleasure of easing Mom's burden, then think of the money she'll be earning. After she's bought a new couch and a refrigerator, she plans to put half of everything she earns in your college funds. That may not thrill you now, but there will come a time when you'll be mighty grateful."

I wondered if Dad was making her go out to work to buy all those things he said she wanted. "Does Mom want to work?" I asked Dad.

"Do you want to work?" Dad asked Mom.

"I assure you, William, that I accepted this job for three reasons. One, I like to teach. Two, I think the work is important, especially now when there will be a shortage of teachers. Three, I am convinced that the members of this family can manage without an undue burden on any one of us. Do you understand?"

I nodded. I understood the words, but I wasn't sure I believed them.

There were changes at school, too. Although Phil Reimer was still the president of the student body, he no longer made the announcements during assembly. The vice president advised us to buy more defense stamps and save our scrap metal. She reminded us that "A slip of a lip could sink a ship." In other words, anyone who knew a secret about anything having to do with the war, where a relative was stationed or what kinds of new equipment we were building, was supposed to keep quiet.

I didn't notice any enemy spies lurking around Plaintown, but I asked my dad about what Clive and Barry had said about the Mennonites spying for Germany.

My dad said those accusations were ridiculous, but he didn't laugh.

Phil Reimer was also the captain of our high school basketball team—for one game. Two seniors on the team had joined the navy during the Christmas vacation, leaving just a few hotshot players. One of these was Phil.

The first game of the season was a home game. We led from the first basket to the last. The stands were filled. The cheerleaders were bouncy. We should have been having a jolly good time, but we weren't.

Phil made the first basket, and I stood up to cheer. I was the only person in my section who stood. The cheering was more like a whisper. I dropped back into my seat, confused. When the other team made a basket, all of their fans cheered. Phil made another basket. Silence. Plaintown fans finally got to their feet and raised their voices when a junior named Cliff scored. The cheers for some and not for Phil made me feel edgy. I was glad the coach benched Phil in the second half when we were ten points ahead.

"Coach has finally wised up," Barry smirked. "We don't need that Nazi-lover on our team."

"You're right about that, Gnat." Clive slapped Barry on the back and grinned at him. Then he turned to me. "What do you think, Silly Willy? You proud of your pal's brother?"

"He made more points than anyone else," I said. "We needed him."

The home crowd, which should have been jumping and shouting after our win, was strangely quiet leaving the gym. Jim and a couple of his friends were just ahead of us as we pushed through the big double doors.

"You and your buddies better start acting like Americans if you know what's good for you," Clive shouted, shaking his fist at Jim's back.

"Right." Barry shook his fist, too.

Phil never shot another basket in the Plaintown High School gym. I don't know if he was asked to quit the team or if he chose to go. We never won another game that season. The only good news was that Allen was moved up to the varsity team. He mostly just practiced with the team, but he played a few minutes in actual games and made a basket in the last game of the season.

I saw Jim in all the classes we took together. Sometimes I said "Hi" or nodded or punched him on the shoulder. Sometimes he did the same. The only time he talked to me was once when he invited me to come skate on his pond. I don't have skates. He offered to find some for me, but I shook my head. He didn't invite me again. I could never think of anything to say to him, which made me sad.

Anne was also sad. She always looked perky at the games. She was a cheerleader; she was supposed to look perky. Other times she seemed to droop like a flower that needed a drink.

One Sunday night she and I arrived for our youth

meeting at the same time. "I hate this war," she muttered as we went down to the basement together.

"It was lousy the way they wouldn't cheer for Phil, wasn't it?"

She took a deep breath and nodded.

"Do you think Phil should buy war bonds and stuff like that?" I asked.

"Not if it's against his religion, I guess. But somebody has to defend our country. What kind of religious freedom would we have if we let the enemy take over America?"

Other kids and the couple who were our sponsors heard her last question.

"We wouldn't have any churches at all," Clive answered.

"We might have churches, but they'd be the ones Hitler or Hirohito chose for us," one of the older guys said.

We discussed the situation for the entire hour, and in the Plaintown Methodist Church at that time we all agreed that it was our duty to defend our country.

"Shouldn't we also defend the rights of the members of the peace churches—the Quakers and Brethren as well as the Mennonites—to practice their religions?" one of the leaders asked.

"We could be like the Pilgrims." Allen laughed. "They came to this country because they wanted religious freedom, and then they insisted that everyone should believe just what they believed."

"What if the Mennonites are right?" Mary Ellen

asked. "What if God meant it when he said, 'Thou shalt not kill,' and 'Blessed are the peacemakers'?"

I liked Mary Ellen. *If I wanted a girlfriend . . .* I thought. *But I didn't. Not yet.*

Climbing the stairs to the sanctuary for evening church, I looked back and saw Anne just standing at the bottom of the steps, staring into space. I stepped away from the crowd and watched her. She shook her shoulders, grabbed the banister, and pulled herself up the stairs like an old lady. When she reached the vestibule, she went to the coatrack and put on her coat. I could tell she was crying.

"Tell my folks I . . ." she said to my dad as she pushed past him and through the big front door.

I got my jacket and followed her. Dad patted my shoulder as I passed him; I was glad he understood. Having caught up with her, I couldn't think of a thing to say, so I just walked along beside her.

I wasn't sure she knew I was there until she spoke. "I love Phil," she said. "I didn't mind that he couldn't go to the homecoming dance. But this is different. Doug and Johnny were probably foolish not to wait until they were graduated, but they thought serving their country was more important than playing basketball or earning diplomas. And Chester. He wrote to me before he went overseas. He said he was scared. I thought that was very brave of him: to admit he was scared." Anne sighed and was silent for a while.

When she spoke again, she sounded angry. "But Phil, who lives on a farm where they have all kinds of scrap metal, won't even bring an old rusty wheel to town. He says he can't promote the war in any way. Sometimes he can be so smug, so sure he's right. He acts like his faith is the only faith—and the rest of us are wrong." Now she sounded furious. "If Hitler drops bombs on us like he does on the British, should we just wait for him to drop more? Phil's way makes no sense at all. Not to me!"

We had reached her front door. "Thanks for walking with me, William, and listening to me." She kissed my cheek. "You're a dear boy."

Why did she have to call me a *dear boy*? That's what my grandmother called me. Anne was only three and a half years older than me. Dear boy, indeed! I made a snowball and threw it with all my might at a yellow stop sign.

"You're home early," Mom said. "Didn't you stay for evening church?"

I went straight upstairs without answering. If she looked at the clock she could see I hadn't been to church. I put on my pajamas and climbed into bed without washing my face or brushing my teeth. I lay on my back with my hands under my head and thought about what people had said at the youth meeting.

Jesus said we had to love one another, including our enemies. How could we love our enemies when they bombed cities and shipped people off to concentration camps? The victims of our enemies needed our love—and our help. I didn't see how we could love both sides. What did God think about this mess? "God is love." That's the first verse every little kid learns in Sunday school. But how could a loving God let people suffer like this?

An unthinkable thought pushed its way into my brain: *What if God doesn't care one way or the other?* It made me uncomfortable when I saw athletic teams praying before a game. If both teams were praying to the same God, how could they expect God to choose one over the other? *What if the war was like a football game to God? Or what if He just wanted to get rid of all the people on the earth and was helping both sides to make bigger and deadlier bombs? Or what if God was nothing more than a folk hero created by people who lived long ago?*

My thoughts were blasphemous. I quickly discarded the idea of sharing them with Dad. Besides, I knew what he would say: *Faith is the substance of things hoped for, the evidence of things not seen.* Thank you, Saint Paul.

Chapter 9

During those first months after the war began, all Americans believed that we would win. As the winter progressed, however, it became more and more obvious that the job was going to be harder and take longer than we had first thought. Attorney General Biddle cautioned the country against underestimating the evil strength of our adversaries. *LIFE* ran maps showing how the United States could be invaded. One map showed the Japs attacking the east coast of Russia, the Aleutian Islands, the coasts of Alaska and Seattle, San Francisco and Los Angeles. Once they'd done that, they'd have control of the aviation industry, shipyards, and oil wells. Then the Germans would land on the East Coast. I didn't present the article to my history class; it was too gloomy.

The next issue of *LIFE* pictured a shell fragment

hurled from a Japanese submarine into an oil field in California and told how a Nazi submarine had torpedoed an oil tanker just eighteen miles off the New Jersey coast. There was also an article about the terrible things the Nazis had done to people in Poland.

My dad always reads the letters to the editor first. The March sixteenth issue had several letters from people who thought the article about Poland should be widely distributed so Americans would know just how evil the enemy was. But one lady made my dad so mad, he threw the magazine across the room. That's something most people don't know about my dad—he has a temper that explodes like a bomb.

"Listen to this stupid woman," he shouted as he picked up the magazine and found his place. "She thinks that war is horrible enough without pictures like the ones from Poland." He changed to a high, prissy voice. "'It seems to me there are brighter sides of life to read about, such as the latest movies, fashions, and plays.'" He returned to his angry voice: "People are being tortured and killed, and she wants to read about fashions. And I bet she calls herself a good Christian. Americans like that . . ."

He stomped out of the room and out of the house. When dad is angry, he usually goes for a long walk to cool down.

The next Sunday he read the letter as part of his sermon about the Good Samaritan and others who cared for one another and bore one another's sorrows.

• • •

My contribution to the war effort seemed pitifully insignificant. We who lived in town didn't have scrap metal to contribute. At our house we filled sacks with flattened tin cans and bundled up our newspapers. Mom poured fat into coffee cans. We tried not to complain about rationing. And even though no one had seen an enemy plane over Kansas, we observed the blackout rules, pulling heavy shades over our windows at night.

Then the March twenty-third issue of *LIFE* arrived with information about something meaningful guys my age could do. The government needed thousands of model planes to be used by spotters in areas where there was danger of an enemy attack and by army and navy gunners to help them learn to estimate a target's distance and speed.

Students were asked to make the models in their woodworking shops. Our high school didn't have a shop, but an old man named Mr. Herbert read the *LIFE* article and offered the use of his shop and his help to any boys who wanted to participate in the project.

At last, I had found a way to contribute to the war effort! About a dozen guys from the Patriots Club signed up, and once we had received the patterns and instructions, we began work, six of us at a time, in Mr. Herbert's basement. I worked Tuesday and Thursday afternoons.

I wanted to go to Mr. Herbert's on Saturday mornings, too, but I had to do housework then. Not only did I have to clean my own room and change my sheets, I had to scrub the bathroom and the kitchen. Dad and I were surely the only males in Plaintown doing "women's work." Dad sang hymns while he vacuumed, which was truly annoying.

We were not invited to Mr. Herbert's on Saturday afternoons, so I usually went to the Roxy with Allen and Barry and other guys from our class. Incidentally, Barry had started walking to and from school with me. He must have received permission from his leader, the Slug.

One by one we began to hear of the deaths of young men from neighboring towns. Then a marine from Plaintown died in the Philippines. I did not know him or any of his family, but I read about him in the two-column article on the front page of the *Plaintown Press*. His name was Merle Lambert. He'd gone to one of the country schools and to our high school. He'd been a member of 4-H and had raised a calf that won a ribbon at the county fair. His teachers remembered him as "a quiet boy."

During the assembly that week, we had a moment of silence in Merle Lambert's honor. After the silence, we sang patriotic songs, as usual, and each class reported on the number of war stamps that had been sold the previous week, as usual, and the Mennonites sat silently with their hands folded in their laps, as usual.

As we were leaving the auditorium, Clive pointed to Jim and shouted, "Hey, Jim! You glad Merle Lambert died? You and your Nazi buddies?"

Jim kept on walking, but his ears turned bright red.

I ran to catch up with Clive. "That's not fair," I said. "Jim can't help it that his family is Mennonite. He's doing what he has to do because he's a member of a Mennonite family."

"You believe that? He and his brothers aren't supporting the war because their mean old daddy won't let his little boys out of his sight? We haven't heard from my brother for weeks, and Jim's brother is sitting around reading books at that Mennonite college in Newton." Clive reached out and grabbed Allen's arm. "Come on, let's leave Silly Willy to cry over those German Mennonites by himself."

Allen pulled his arm away from Clive and walked to class with me—which felt very good, let me tell you.

The next week Clive started calling Jim *schlecht Junge,* which he said meant "bad boy" in German.

One noon when we went to lunch, we saw that German swastikas had been painted on the two tables where the Mennonite kids always ate their lunches. We watched silently while the Mennonites went together to the kitchen and came back with a couple of damp rags and scouring powder. Each kid took a turn scrubbing until the swastikas had disappeared. Together, they marched back to the kitchen with their tools, and back to their tables. They sat down and bowed their heads for a few minutes before they ate.

When I told my dad about the swastikas, he blew up, right there at the dinner table; he even swore.

"What the hell is this world coming to?" He banged his fist on the table so that the silverware jumped.

"Please, Bill," my mother said in the low, distinct voice that means you'd better listen to her.

"Yesss." Dad got up from the table and strode to the kitchen. We could hear him pacing back and forth across the kitchen floor. The pacing stopped. The water ran and was turned off. On. Off. And then Dad was standing in the doorway, gulping down a tall glass of water. Finally he returned to the table. "Sorry that I swore and banged the table." He picked up his fork, and we all finished our dinner in silence.

"May I be excused?" Maggie spoke in the little voice that meant she was still frightened.

"Sure, Pumpkin." Dad smiled at her. As soon as she was standing, he pulled her toward him, kissed her cheek, and sent her on her way with a pat on her bottom.

"May I be excused?" Darlene pushed back her chair.

"No, you may not be excused. Nor you, William." Dad glared at us. "We are going to talk about swastikas. They are the symbol of evil, of the massacre of innocent people, of everything that Jesus condemned and we must also condemn. We may not agree with the Mennonite position on war, but that does not make their position wrong. Remember that. Now let's pray."

I stared at him for a moment. We pray before dinner; he'd already blessed the food. Mother tapped her foot against mine, and I bowed my head while

Dad prayed that we might all demonstrate the love of God in our little town and that the war might end quickly. He also prayed for the suffering people of the world.

When he had said "Amen" and raised his head, he spoke directly to me. "Remember, it is often easier to love the suffering people of Greece or Africa whom we do not know, than to love the people we do know who don't agree with us. You may clear the table now."

I was not surprised Sunday morning when the scripture reading was from the Beatitudes:

"'Blessed are the peacemakers: for they shall be called the children of God. . . . Blessed are ye, when men shall revile you, and persecute you, and shall say all manner of evil against you falsely, for my sake . . .'"

What did surprise me was that in addition to the Scripture, he read the part of the Constitution that guarantees religious freedom. The biggest surprise came when he announced that he had gone out to visit "my friend, Dick Reimer." He talked about how the Mennonites had been good neighbors in our community since the 1870s and pacifists for more than four centuries.

Dad said that the peace churches—the Mennonites, Quakers, and Brethren—were setting up camps where conscientious objectors, which is what pacifists were called, could serve humanity without contributing to the war. Men in several camps in the Midwest were working on soil conservation projects. Dad said that

Kansas farmers, who had suffered through the dust storms just a few years back, could certainly appreciate that work.

A few Mennonites felt that the work in camps was too close to war work, because the men who worked there freed other men to fight. Those few were prepared to go to prison if necessary.

A third acceptable alternative for conscientious objectors was to serve in a noncombat role in the regular army. They could be medics and ambulance drivers. They did not carry guns, making their work especially dangerous, Dad said.

After church, Clive followed me through the Sunday school rooms to the back door. "So your dad's an enemy sympathizer. Are you planning to dodge the draft, too? You and your Mennonite pals."

He turned to go back through the sanctuary, but I grabbed his belt and growled at him from behind. "My dad is as patriotic as any person in this town. And Jim and his friends are doing what they have to do. So button your lip. Hear me?" I let go of his belt and gave him a shove.

Spring came at last, and I longed to find a way to be friends with Jim. My reasons were selfish. I wanted to go fishing with him. I wanted to go on the camping trips we'd planned.

Maybe Jim wanted to support the war effort. *Friends tell friends things.* Why didn't he tell me how he felt? I began saying, "Hello," and, "Did you finish your homework?" hoping that he'd say, *William, there's something I want to tell you.* I even asked him how he was feeling. He said he felt fine; he was talking about his body, not his heart.

Chapter 10

Phil Reimer didn't wait for the graduation ceremony but went to one of the soil conservation camps the day after his last exam. The pitcher of the baseball team took Anne Armstrong to the prom and left the next day for Camp Riley. Anne went off to work in a summer camp; in the fall she would go to a women's college in Missouri.

And me? I was born too late to fly a war plane, to take Anne Armstrong to a dance, to get a real job. Kids just a little older than me could be soda jerks at the drugstore or they could deliver groceries. But I was still fourteen. The only job I could get would be lawn mowing–now and then–for pennies. I planned to spend a big part of my summer at Mr. Herbert's making model planes. That wouldn't put money in my pocket, but it was worthwhile and something I was good at.

Those were my summer plans until the Sunday of the last week of school. As we came out of church, one of the deacons called to me. He'd never said more than "hello" to me in all the months we'd lived in Plaintown. "You know how to drive a tractor?" he asked.

I shook my head, bewildered. And then it came to me: Mr. Jacobsen was said to have a big wheat farm. "I could learn. I'm a fast learner."

He looked me over silently while I stood as tall as I could. "I've grown at least three inches since fall, and I'd work hard, Mr. Jacobsen."

Suddenly he grinned—so wide that I could see the gaps behind the four front teeth in his lower jaw. "We'll give it a try. You're young, but with my two boys in the navy and all the hired men in the area off to make their fortunes in defense work, I can't afford to be choosy now, can I? I need help a few days a week except during harvest, when I'd expect you to work ten or twelve hours a day, six days a week. That's a lot for a lad your age."

"I can do it, Mr. Jacobsen."

He clamped his hand down hard on my shoulder and told me to come out to his farm as soon as the school year ended. He would pay me fifty cents an hour, plus a bonus if the harvest was good. He said he'd spoken to my dad.

He hadn't spoken to my mom, but Dad reminded her that these were special times that called for special employment. He was serving two churches, she was teaching school, I would be helping put bread on the tables of America. I tried to remember that on

afternoons when my whole body ached. *I am putting bread on the tables of America.*

Unless God sent us too much rain or too little rain or hail or some other disaster, we would indeed have a great harvest, according to Jim Reimer's reports. Now I'm going to tell you about Kansas wheat. If you think my report is boring, remember that I had to sit through a similar report every week.

You probably think that crops are planted in the spring and harvested in the fall. True, for corn and alfalfa and oats. Also true for some wheat now, and for all wheat until the 1870s. That's when the Mennonites brought winter wheat from Russia to Kansas. It's called "winter wheat" because it is planted in September and grows until frost, sending down deep roots that survive the winter. Come spring it grows tall, and the heads of grain form.

I have heard people say that Kansas is ugly—the land is flat, and there aren't many trees or rivers. The weather can be extreme, like an oven in summer and an icebox in winter. But before the wheat harvest in June, Kansas turns to gold, "amber waves of grain," like in the song.

Last fall and winter had been almost perfect for the wheat: enough rain and no frost until late in the year. In the spring of 1942 people in town were saying, "Wheat's looking good," and the farmers were doing what my dad says Kansas farmers always do, grumping. "Watch out for the green bugs," one of them would warn. "Remember the freeze in May of thirty-eight,

and the Hessian fly last year." No farmer would ever say, "Boy, this is going to be one great year." Farmers are superstitious. They think that one way to be sure you'll have a lousy crop is to expect a good one.

The first Monday morning after the last day of school, I rode my rusty old bike out to the Jacobsens'. Along the way, I studied the wheat fields, prayed for a good harvest, and thought about the bike I would buy as soon as I'd earned the money for it.

I worked three days that week. I cleaned the chicken house, which is one stinky job, let me tell you. I also hoed weeds in Mrs. Jacobsen's garden, and helped Mr. Jacobsen oil the machinery and repair a fence. The best hours were those I spent learning to drive the tractor.

I worked half a day on Saturday, collected my pay, and went to the picture show with Barry and two other guys from our class. Allen was at his grandfather's farm in Nebraska, and Clive had gone to his family's cabin in the Colorado Rockies. Clive had made that cabin sound mighty inviting, especially to someone like me, who had never been anywhere. I'm still waiting to see a mountain and an ocean.

It was so steamy inside the Roxy that the seat felt like a scratchy blanket wrapped around my body. I left as soon as the credits came on the screen, and went straight to Schultz's hardware store to look at bikes. Barry tagged along.

Saturday is the busiest day of the week for store keepers in Plaintown, but Mr. Schultz had no customers.

His shelves were partially empty, and there wasn't a single bike on display.

When Mr. Schultz asked if he could help me, I said, "No, thank you," and started toward the door. Then I turned back. "No bikes? I'm working for Jake Jacobsen. I was counting on buying a bike this summer."

"Like that black one you were mooning over just before Christmas? It's not going to be easy to find a bike just like that. Or any bike. Bike manufacturers have already begun to convert their plants to make war goods." He all but spit out the words "war goods." Then he sighed. "But there are still some to be had, though they'll be more expensive. Tell me what you're looking for, and I'll see what I can find for you, William."

"I don't have enough money yet," I explained. Mr. Jacobsen had paid me $11.50 for twenty-three hours of work, but I had to give a tenth to the church and save half for war bonds. The movie had cost a quarter, and I'd bought popcorn and candy. I pulled four one-dollar bills out of my pocket and put them on the counter beside the cash register. "I'll have more next week," I bragged. "Lots more."

Mr. Schultz laughed. "Then I'll try to find a bike for you. You can pay for it week by week. What did you have in mind?" He took a pencil out of his pocket and pulled a piece of wrapping paper toward him while I hesitated.

I thought of Clive's bike. I wanted one like it but not *exactly* like it.

Mr. Schultz seemed to read my mind. "You want a high quality bike that will hold up on our rough roads and will provide dependable transportation until you can get a car of your own. Right?"

"Right. With a basket and reflectors. I'd like a leather seat, but . . ."

"What color? Better not be too choosy; we may just have to take what we can get."

"Black," Barry said.

"Any color *but* black," I snapped. "Any shade of red or blue. Green? Yellow? But not black."

We discussed the wheel size and agreed that I should have a slightly too-big bike since I was still growing.

"I'm going to get a new bike," Barry announced as we were walking along Main Street toward home. "Yellow. But I won't get it from Schultz. I'll buy mine from a true-blue American. My dad's working in a big airplane plant in California. He sent us a check just last week. He's going to send money so I can get a new bike."

"Great!" Secretly, I had my doubts about Barry's dad. I'd never seen him. "Maybe your dad will get a job in Wichita. Then you could see him often."

"Nah. Pay's better in California. But he'll come for a visit soon. He wants to see us." We stopped in front of my house. Barry ran his hand through his black curls and tugged at his shirt. "Did you know that guys who don't begin to grow until they are older grow taller? By the time we graduate from high school, I'll be looking down on the top of your head."

Before I could say anything, he had run on through

our yard to the alley. I asked my mom about what Barry had said.

"Poor Barry." She sighed. "You used to be just a little taller than him. He must have hated it when you began to grow, but some boys do grow late in their teens."

The next week I worked two and a half days. Saturday morning, as soon as I'd finished my chores, I went to the hardware store. Mr. Schultz met me at the door and led me into his back room, where he pulled the light chain to illuminate not one but two Schwinn bikes, both of them beauties. I tested the grips on the handlebars, worked the pedals with my hands, ran my fingers down the smooth, shiny fenders.

"Better give them each a test run," Mr. Schultz said, opening the door to the alley."

I rode to the end of the alley and back on the dark blue bike and to the end of the alley and back on the maroon bike. I parked them side by side, just where they had been before. Still, I hadn't said one word.

"So? Do you like either of these?" His eyes twinkled so that I knew that he knew the answer to that question. How could any kid not like either of the bikes?

"They are glorious, great, fabulous, terrific. Both of them."

"They're also expensive. Just as I feared, prices have gone up since the war. The blue one will be thirty-nine dollars; the red one—you see it has a suede saddle and a horn and a light—is forty-five."

A lot of money! I'd have to work almost one hundred hours to earn the red one. I started to choose the blue one. No! I chose the bike of my dreams. Mr. Schultz wheeled the blue bike to the front of the store and put it in the window. He put my name on a big piece of wrapping paper and draped it over the dark red bike to keep it clean.

I gave Mr. Schultz seven dollars. Each week after that I made a payment on my bike, and each week Mr. Schultz gave me a receipt.

Chapter 11

During the harvest of 1942 I learned the meaning of the words "bone tired." On the Sunday afternoon before we began the harvest, I moved into Don Jacobsen's bedroom. The first night I looked at all of the pictures of ships he had taped up on his walls. He loved ships just as much as I loved planes. He had earned letters in track and baseball and a trophy for winning the broad jump at an all-state meet. I hadn't met Don Jacobsen, but I was proud to be filling his shoes on the home front.

When I climbed into his bed, I thought I'd never be able to sleep on such a hard mattress. Every night after that, Don's bed and Don's room were the most welcome sights on the farm.

We were up at daybreak, and we worked until sunset, six and a half days a week. We worked Sunday afternoon and the Fourth of July. When we had harvested all of Jacobsen's wheat, we moved to the fields planted by the farmers who were helping us. One belonged to the old man who drove one of the trucks. The other to a man who came with his nine-year-old kid. The kid was the water boy.

I drove the tractor that pulled the combine. The combine is a long machine that cuts the wheat a few inches from the ground and cuts the heads off the stalks. Then it separates the grain from the chaff and shoots the grain into a truck. When the truck is full, the driver takes it to the elevator in town, and another driver brings another truck alongside the combine.

The sun beat down on us every day during that harvest, and the daytime temperature never dropped below ninety degrees. I wore a hat and a long-sleeved shirt, but the back of my neck and the backs of my hands were burned to the color of smoked ham.

During the harvest Mr. Jacobsen's wife and their two daughters, both older than me, and the wife of their older son, Bob, did all the chores and made huge meals. We had ham and eggs and fried potatoes for breakfast. And chicken or beef or pork and vegetables and Jell-O salads and pies and cakes for our noon meal. I can't remember what we ate in the evening. I only remember that on the second day of harvest my forehead dropped into a bowl of potato salad. Everyone laughed, and I stayed awake through the evening meals after that. It wasn't easy, let me tell you. I always went to sleep as soon as the meal was over—never mind how hard the bed had felt that first night.

During the whole of those two weeks it never rained a single drop, for which every farmer in the county was grateful—and every storekeeper and banker. Even the minister and doctor were grateful. When times are bad, doctors and ministers are often paid in chickens and eggs and potatoes, if they are paid at all. Once, when my dad was serving his first church, he wasn't paid money for several months. He and Mom had to eat whatever the members of their church gave them. One week they received nothing but eggs. Mom said they had poached eggs for breakfast, egg salad for lunch, and an omelet for dinner. A good harvest meant that my dad would receive regular checks from both of his churches.

We finished the harvest at noon on Saturday of the second week. Before every noon meal Mr. Jacobsen had said a one-sentence grace: "Make us ever grateful for this food we are about to receive and watch over Bob and Don. Amen." The day the harvest ended he prayed on and on, thanking God for the fine weather and the wheat and the men and boys who had harvested the wheat. He asked God's blessing on the "womenfolk" who had done double duty in the kitchen and the barns. He prayed for all the boys who were serving their country and especially for Don and Bob. And then he prayed for all the ill and hungry people in wartorn countries around the world.

We all said, "Amen."

We ate more slowly and talked more than at any previous meal. Bob's wife read parts of a letter she had received from her husband: "'I'm real sorry not to be there to help with the harvest. Can't believe you'll be able to bring it all in on time without Don and me.'"

"You tell him that we got along okay without him," Mr. Jacobsen said. "Tell him that William and I and our neighbors and you womenfolk did the job and did it just fine." He paused. "But tell him we all missed him and Don."

Mr. Jacobsen drove me home. On the way to town he discussed my pay. "I figure you worked twelve hours a day six days a week and one-half day on Sunday. I figure that was one hundred fifty hours."

"I only worked four hours today," I said.

"Never mind, William. You've been a good worker. I appreciate that you never complained, even when I could see that you were tired enough to fall off that tractor—or into the potato salad. I promised you a bonus if the harvest was good. Of course, prices are down this year. . . ." *Kansas farmers always complain, no matter how good their situation.* "Still, prices aren't too bad. And it was a decent harvest."

Decent? I'd read in the paper that it could be the best harvest in decades.

Mr. Jacobsen left me standing just inside the bank while he went up to one of the tellers. Clive's uncle was at his big polished desk behind a railing. He was talking with two men who sat opposite him, but he looked up and nodded to me.

Mr. Jacobsen came away from the teller with a stack of bills and handed me the top one, a twenty. And another twenty, and another, and another, and another. One hundred dollars! Mom didn't make one hundred dollars in two weeks, and Dad didn't either!

I thanked Mr. Jacobsen and put the bills in my shoe. Out on the sidewalk, I ran straight down Maine Street toward the hardware store, picturing myself riding my new bike back up Maine Street to the parsonage. I'd ride slowly, giving everyone a chance to admire the shiny finish and the beautiful color and the minister's kid who not only had a new bike but the very best new bike—which he had earned himself.

I was just two storefronts from my destination when I stopped, dismayed. Where was the barrel of garden tools and brooms that Mr. Schultz rolled out onto the sidewalk every morning? I closed my eyes as I approached the window. Then I forced them open. It was just as I feared: Mr. Schultz's store was empty. The door was locked. And my bike? Where was my bike?

I turned and ran, dodging the people on the sidewalk, afraid to speak to any of them for fear I might start bawling like a newborn calf. That bike was so important to me!

"Where you going in such a hurry?" Barry shouted behind me. "Wait up."

I didn't stop.

"What's the matter with you?" Barry said, panting. "You think you're better than everybody else just because you had a job? Why don't you slow down?"

Without a word I ran on, past our church and up the walk to our house.

"You're home." Mom came running from the kitchen, holding her arms wide. "Welcome home, William."

I pushed past her and ran up the stairs and threw myself across my bed.

I heard Mom asking Barry if he knew what was wrong. And then I heard the clatter of the lawn mower—Dad was in the backyard. Still breathless, I ran down the stairs, dodging around Mom and Barry and letting the screen door slam behind me.

"Mr. Schultz stole my bike," I shouted to Dad, and then, wanting to be honest, I added, "Actually he stole part of my bike, the part I've already paid for. But today I went to get my bike with the one hundred dollars Mr. Jacobsen gave me—can you believe that he gave me one hundred dollars, Dad?—and Mr. Schultz has closed his store and gone away and—"

"And you jump to conclusions, completely unfounded conclusions." Dad was mad. I could see that in his eyes. He took off his hat and mopped his head with a dirty handkerchief, all the time staring at me. "What makes you think that Mr. Schultz would cheat you, William?"

Barry was tiptoeing across the backyard to the alley while I hung my head.

"Wait, Barry," Dad said. "Hear the truth."

"Mr. Schultz has closed his store," Barry whispered.

"And my bike is gone," I added.

"Your bike is not gone. Mr. Schultz had to close his store because unthinking people like you, people who jump to conclusions, wouldn't buy there anymore. He couldn't afford to pay the rent on the store, so he's sold his house in town and moved out to the country, among his own people. He moved what was left in the store to a barn out there, except for one bicycle, which he delivered here."

"Here? Where did you put it?" I started toward the house.

"Stop," Dad commanded. "I offered to pay Mr. Schultz the rest of what you owed on the bike, but he said, 'Oh no, this was a business deal with William. I know he'll pay me when he has the money. No hurry.' He trusted you, William, and you? I'm disgusted that my son . . . could . . . oh, William, how could you be so unfair, so utterly un-Christian? Jesus said, 'Judge not, that ye be not judged.' How could you forget that verse?" Dad turned his back on me. "Go on home, Barry," he said.

I was glad when Barry left, because I almost cried. Truth? I did cry. If a cyclone had suddenly swept me up into the clouds, I'd have been grateful.

"Go to your room," Dad said. "When I've had a chance to think this through, I'll come and tell you what your punishment will be. Right now I'd like to beat the tar out of you."

I had fallen asleep, but I woke when Dad came into my room. Without speaking he handed me a slip of paper noting the cost of the bike, my payments, and the amount due. At the bottom, Mr. Schultz had written, *I hope this fine bike gives you much pleasure.*

Why hadn't he written something nasty? *Pay up, kid, or I'll send the sheriff after you.*

"Mr. Jacobsen paid you one hundred dollars," Dad said in his I-will-not-tolerate-any-nonsense-from-you voice. "That's a lot of money. I don't know how you were planning to spend it, but I'll tell you how you *will* spend it. Tomorrow you're going to put ten dollars in this church envelope and put it in the collection. I don't want your name on the envelope. You will give it in secret, not bragging about your riches. Monday you will ride out to Mr. Schultz's place and pay what you owe."

"I'll apologize to him," I said.

"You will not. An apology might make you feel better, but do you really think that Mr. Schultz needs to know that you thought he had cheated you? You'll do your apologizing to God, in this room, which you will not leave except to go to church tomorrow. The bike is in the basement, but you will not look at it until Monday. Also on Monday you will take the rest of your earnings, and whatever earnings you have left from previous weeks, and you and I will buy war bonds and stamps with every dollar and dime. When you get ready for college, you'll be glad to have that money. In the meantime, no ice cream or picture shows or any other treats until you earn more money. Have I made myself clear?"

I nodded, too miserable to speak.

"I know you're sorry. I just hope you'll be more careful about jumping to conclusions in the future. It's always wise to give everyone the benefit of the doubt until you have proof that what you think to be true is true."

Dad sat quietly on my bed for a minute or two and then he got up and patted my shoulder. "By the way, William, Mr. Jacobsen stopped by with your suitcase. He said you'd worked like a man every day for two weeks without ever complaining. That made me and your mother proud." He left the room, closing the door quietly.

Dad's final speech made me feel even worse.

The harvest must have left me more tired than I had thought. I had supper alone in my room. No dessert. Then I opened the Zane Grey novel I'd asked Mom to get for me at the library. I read the first page—and fell asleep. I woke up to go to the bathroom and changed to my pajama bottom—it was too hot to wear the top—and then slept until Dad brought me my orange juice and cornflakes.

I didn't want to talk to Barry, so I made sure I was late arriving for my Sunday school class. Then I was sorry I hadn't come earlier, because the church basement was the coolest place I had been in the last two weeks.

There was no way I could avoid Barry. He came up the stairs between Sunday school and church with me. "You going out to pay Schultz tomorrow?" he asked. "I'll ride out with you. Maybe take our lunches . . . "

"No." I didn't want Barry and his big, bigoted mouth with me. "I have to go alone."

He looked puzzled for a moment, then he shrugged his shoulders and ran on up to the balcony.

All the windows and doors were open in the sanctuary, and there were big electric fans on either side of the altar. In the pews we tried to create a breeze with the cardboard fans that had been placed in the hymnbook racks by the Plaintown funeral home.

The choir didn't sing during the summer—it was too hot up there in the choir loft—but a lady with a quavery voice sang a solo while I thought about Anne Armstrong at the camp where she was working. Dad was not wearing his suit jacket, but his tie was knotted high under his stiff white shirt collar. He kept mopping his forehead, and I could see growing circles of sweat under his arms.

Back in my bedroom it was so hot I imagined myself melting into a puddle. *What's that greasy pool doing in William's room,* someone would ask. *Oh, that?* Dad would laugh. *That's William himself. Didn't you notice his glasses floating on top?*

I tore a cover from *LIFE* and folded it accordion style. I put my book against the screen in the only window in my prison and knelt in front of it, fanning my face as I read. Late in the afternoon God finally sent a natural breeze.

Chapter 12

Early Monday morning, before the stores along Main Street had opened, I was cruising through town on my super-smooth swift bike. It glided over the cracks in the pavement.

I had expected my first ride on my new bike to be south to the Jacobsens'. Instead, I was heading north on the road that passed Jim's farm. I made a discovery that morning: Mennonites drive black cars. Don Jacobsen had a flashy red convertible, which his father kept covered in the barn and started every week just to be sure it would be in good shape when Don came home. The Jacobsens' family car was green, and the truck had a yellow cab. Phil Reimer and Mr. Reimer and Jim's cousins all drove black cars. Many of the farms I passed that morning were Mennonite farms.

The clothes Mennonite kids wore were like their cars, neat but drab. The girls didn't wear lipstick. I wondered if dull was part of Jim's religion.

I had been instructed to turn left at the one-room elementary school six miles out of town. Long before I reached it, the morning breezes and the fluffy clouds disappeared. The sun rose high and hot. I began to sweat so that my shirt clung to my back, and drops rolled down my forehead into my eyes. The pedals moved slowly as if the flat road were a steep hill. Water shimmered across the highway ahead, a wicked mirage.

At last I saw the schoolhouse—and the pitcher pump near the door. I rode into the yard, jumped off my bike, and began to pump. As soon as water flowed, I knelt and soaked my head. Then I pumped water into my hand and gulped the little my hand could hold, again and again.

Cooled, I pedaled along the dirt road and into the lane beyond the Schultz mailbox. On one side of the lane was a big white farmhouse; on the other side was a little cottage with peeling white paint. Mr. Schultz was hammering shingles on the roof of the cottage.

When he saw me, he hurried down the ladder, greeted me like an old friend, and accepted the money I owed him. I told him how much I liked the bike and how smooth my ride had been, and I thanked him for getting it for me and for delivering it before I had paid for it. All the time, I was wishing I could apologize or, better yet, that he had been stiff and cold. Instead, he patted me on the shoulder and invited me into his house, where Mrs. Schultz nodded and smiled at me. She did not speak.

"She was born and raised in Germany," Mr. Schultz explained. "It embarrasses her that her English is not perfect—actually, it's far better than my German."

She set glasses of lemonade and big molasses cookies on the table and said, in English, "Please sit."

Mr. Schultz explained that he, too, had been helping with the harvest and hadn't had a chance to work on his house until that morning. "But this little house will be nice and snug and suit us just fine," he said.

Mrs. Schultz nodded. "I not like town. Not now."

Not now, when people are being nasty to us, is what she meant. She couldn't have wanted to leave their much larger house in town. After living with electric lights and a radio and maybe even a modern refrigerator, she would certainly find it difficult to do without them.

"My people. Very bad in Germany." She turned to her husband. "Tell him."

"She wants you to know that people in her country are suffering. All men, even the very young and the pacifists, are forced into the army and forced to carry guns. Old men and women and children are destitute."

I didn't know what to say, so I said I had to get home. I gulped down my lemonade, thanked Mr. and Mrs. Schultz, said good-bye, and sped down the lane to the main road.

I couldn't believe that these people were actually *sympathizing* with the enemy. But the Germans were not enemies of Mrs. Schultz; some of them were family to her. *Who did Mrs. Schultz want to win this war? The Germans? That could not be.* People who sympathized with the enemy spied on our military bases and sabotaged our shipyards. They were traitors. But Mr. Schultz seemed like such a nice man. Surely *he* wanted America to win the war, even if he couldn't— or wouldn't—do his part.

I was so upset by these thoughts that I peddled right past the schoolhouse. My brain was boiling. Finally I realized that my body was also steaming, and my throat was dry. When I came to the Reimers', I turned into their lane and peddled straight to their pitcher pump.

"Come to show me that fancy bike?" Jim asked, grinning broadly as he came out of the barn.

I was grinning too, and thinking how much I missed him and his crazy eyebrow. "I bought it with the money I made working for Jake Jacobsen." I told him about my job while I put my bike on the kickstand and mopped my forehead with my shirtsleeve.

Jim went to the pump and began to work the handle, motioning me to put my head under the spout. I knelt there on all fours while cool water soaked my head. When I started to drink out of my hand, Jim stopped pumping, and we went into the kitchen where I gulped down three glasses of water.

"I've been out to Mr. Scuhltz's to pay the last of

what I owed on my bike." I thought Jim would like to know that I was not one of the people who had boycotted Schultz's store. "He got it for me in Hutchinson. I'm grateful for that."

We were sitting on the porch when a little pig walked across the yard, put her hoofs on the bottom step, and stretched up to nuzzle Jim's hand, just like a dog.

Jim scratched the pig between its ears. "Name's Pee-Wee. Runt of the litter. I bottle-fed her." Jim laughed. "Thinks I'm her mother."

For a while neither of us said anything. I thought about how long it had been since I'd talked with Jim. I didn't even know he'd adopted a pig. I wondered how Jim's old dog, Max, took to the new pet.

"Max died. Didn't wake up one morning. Buried him over there." He nodded toward the corncrib.

How did Jim know I was thinking about his dog? Could he read my mind?

I decided to ask him about Mennonite cars and Mennonite clothes. "Am I right that most of your cars are black?"

He nodded and laughed. "Sometimes dark blue. We live simply and humbly. But some of us are more simple and humble than others."

Then he told me that there are some Mennonites who don't drive cars at all. Some are so sure that decoration of any kind is wrong that the men don't have collars on their jackets. When electricity eventually became available to the farms in central Kansas, the

Mennonites would have to decide if electric appliances were or were not "sinful."

"And your family? What will your family decide, Jim?"

"I don't know. We don't talk about it much. It won't be an issue until after the war. Then I expect we will decide that electricity is a gift from God; some of our neighbors may think it is a temptation sent by the devil." He laughed, and I laughed with him, thinking how good it felt to sit there beside my good friend Jim.

"Those Mennonites think that we are too modern. You think we are old-fashioned because we don't dance and our girls don't wear lipstick."

He was right. I did think he was old-fashioned, but I didn't care what color his car was or what he wore. I only wanted him to be a patriotic American.

"Mrs. Schultz has relatives in Germany," I said. "She's worried about them."

"Many of us have people in Germany."

"But you want America to win this war, right?"

"We want the war to be over and the killing to stop. Our people in Germany are not Nazis. They never supported Hitler."

Of course, they didn't. But what did they do to stop Hitler? We sat in silence while I thought about the question I really wanted to ask. Finally I spoke. "When we went camping, you said that friends tell friends things, but . . ."

"Go ahead." His crazy eyebrow shot up almost to

his hairline so I knew that he was worried that I might ask a question he didn't want to answer.

I hesitated, searching for the right words. "In your heart of hearts, do you wish you could support the war effort, Jim? Would you, if your folks would let you?"

"When I'm eighteen, I might do what Paul is doing. He joined the army. Did you know that? The medics. He won't be fighting, but he'll be helping those who are."

"Why didn't Phil do that? He could wear a uniform. Be part of things." The medics seemed to me to be the perfect solution for guys who thought it was wrong to fight. Soil conservation seemed like something anyone could work at—old folks, women—and boring.

"Phil doesn't want to wear a uniform or be part of the army. He says the army is a killing machine."

"And your dad? What did he tell your brothers to do?"

"He said they were adults and had to decide for themselves what they thought was right."

"And you, Jim? What would you like to do now? Would you like to bring in scrap metal and buy bonds and sing patriotic songs?"

He stared at me and said nothing while I began to wish I hadn't asked. Finally he spoke. "War is wrong. All war. We can't pick our wars."

"But Hitler has been killing innocent people, trying to conquer all of Europe. Mrs. Schultz said that he's making it hard on the people in his own country. If enough people had tried, don't you think they could have stopped Hitler and the Nazis before they marched into Poland, before the blitz? Couldn't they have saved thousands of lives?"

Jim didn't say anything, which made me believe that he thought I was right.

I continued my argument. "The czar kicked your grandmother out of Russia—and America took her in. That must make a difference to you." He started to speak, but I interrupted him. "You must *want* to be a patriotic American, Jim. I won't tell anyone. I'd just like to know what you really think, in your heart of hearts."

He stood up and made a fist, which he pressed into his own chest. "I, me, Jim Reimer, I believe that war is wrong. All war. I wish that everyone felt the same way. Then no one would fight. I'm not sure that Paul was right to join the army. Maybe Phil made the best decision. I do know that we Mennonites have a responsibility to show the rest of the world that it is possible to live in peace with our neighbors. We're not interested in countries and boundaries; we're interested in people—and their relationship to God. We are upset about war hurting anyone, anywhere."

"So what are you doing to stop this war?" When I heard the anger in my own voice, I tried to grin it away.

"I am praying, and I am reminding myself that two wrongs do not make a right." He sounded like a pious old lady. Even his eyebrow seemed to have changed, making his face look evil.

I jumped up. Anger, like a bolt of electricity, darted between us.

"'Love your enemies, bless them that curse you, do good to them that hate you,'" Jim murmured.

I headed toward my bike. He didn't need to quote Scripture to me. "'Be ye therefore perfect, even as your Father which is in heaven is perfect,'" I shouted, to demonstrate that I knew as many Bible verses as he did. And I was just as good a Christian and I could hardly wait to fly over enemy territory and drop bombs on America's enemies.

After lunch, I took all my money to the bank, where I bought bonds. Then I rode to Mr. Herbert's. He had invited any boys who wanted to work on the plane project to come to his house Monday through Friday afternoons during the summer. Before the harvest I had been there most days that I hadn't been working at the Jacobsens'. I was glad to be back making models that would help our flyers and our gunners. That gave me pleasure. I wished Jim could see me doing my part to win the war.

Chapter 13

I continued to work two or three days a week for Mr. Jacobsen. Right after the harvest we plowed the wheat fields. Later that summer we disked the fields several times to prepare the soil for the wheat that would be planted in September. I drove the tractor that pulled the disk, which cut the weeds and broke up the soil so that any rain would soak in, not run off.

I also helped mend fences. All too often I had to clean that miserable henhouse. Oh, how I hated that job! Actually, I hate chickens until they are brought to the table on a platter. It's a miracle that anything so ugly can taste so good.

Every weekday that I did not work, I built model planes. Two guys spent every afternoon at the Herberts'. One was a fat kid with thick glasses and pimples named Dwight. He would be a junior in the fall. The other was

Mr. Herbert's next-door neighbor, Danny, who would be a freshman. He'd had polio when he was five and was always in his wheelchair.

Allen had worked on his grandfather's farm in Nebraska through the harvest. After he came home he pumped gas at his cousin's station a few mornings a week. Most afternoons he also came to Mr. Herbert's. Barry and a few others came now and then.

The first to arrive would bring the pieces and tools up from the basement to the picnic table under an oak tree. It was cooler there than any other place in town. We'd listen to a ball game on the radio or just talk while we sawed and sanded and glued and painted. In the middle of the afternoon Mrs. Herbert or Danny's mother usually brought us something to drink.

Late in the afternoon a couple of the guys played chess. Mr. Herbert taught the game to Allen and me—and Barry, when he could sit still, which wasn't often.

The second week after harvest Clive rode his black and silver bike into Mr. Herbert's driveway and across the lawn, stopping next to the table. He straddled the bar on his bike, and I noticed that his hair was almost as white as Santa's and his face was as red. His nose and forehead were peeling.

"You guys think you're doing something for the war effort? Let me tell you what I've been doing. I worked all day every day for four weeks. Before the war, Chester didn't have to work all day during harvest, but the peasants depend on Van Dyne's elevator, and this year help was short. So the heir apparent–that's me–had to fill in."

Barry tittered as if Clive's bragging was amusing.

"But don't you guys worry about me. I'm off to the mountains again to cool off and fish and swim and putt around in our boat. There are some mighty good-looking girls up there. It'll be my duty to fill Chester's shoes by entertaining a few of them myself." He pretended to sweep a hat from his head as he bowed low over the side of the crossbar of his bike. "Clive Van Dyne to the rescue."

Again, Barry tittered. "Want to take me along?"

"Not you, Gnat. You stay here and play with your model planes." He started to pedal away and then stopped. "So what's with this red bike?"

"It's mine," I said.

"Yours? Preacher's Brat has a shiny new bike? Who'd you steal it from?"

I'd been feeling angry with Clive from the minute he rode over the Herberts' lawn. I rose to my feet and climbed over the bench and went to face Clive. My fist was clenched.

"Great bike, isn't it?" Dwight was standing beside me. "William earned the money working at the Jacobsens'. Their boys are in the navy."

"Old Man Jacobsen hired a pip-squeak like Silly Willy Four-Eyes? I don't believe it."

"You think William is a pip-squeak? He looks about average height to me." Dwight was right. I was not as tall as Allen and Clive, but I was much taller than Barry and about the same height as Dwight.

"Have it your way, Fatso." Clive peddled off.

"Disagreeable young man, isn't he?" Dwight laughed.

"A braggart." I slapped Dwight on the shoulder so he would know I knew that he had saved me from my own temper.

"He's rich," Barry said. "He has a boat and—"

"And a lousy personality," Dwight inserted.

Barry was a sloppy worker. We let him do the first sanding—somebody had to do it—but I or one of the other guys always had to finish the sanding before his pieces could be glued and painted.

Barry was also a pest. When we got out the chessboards, he really annoyed me. Instead of trying to learn the game, he made silly moves. He'd jump his pawn, which can only move one square at a time, all the way across the board and shout, "Checkmate." He thought that was funny. Some days he'd swing his legs and kick his opponent.

Danny was a better player than me, but one day after the opening moves, it seemed that I might win a game from him—until Barry released the brake on the wheelchair. The chair moved forward, and the board, which we had balanced on our knees, flipped over, scattering the men across the lawn.

"Sit still or go home," I shouted at Barry.

He went home and he didn't come back any afternoon during the rest of the summer.

• • •

Early in August a reporter from the *Plaintown Press* came to Mr. Herbert's to find out more about the model plane project. She asked questions and took pictures.

On Thursday when Mr. Jacobsen and I went to the house for the noon meal, the *Press* was propped up between the salt and pepper shakers in the middle of the table. On the front page was a two-column picture of Dwight and Danny and me and some of our planes.

When we'd finished our dessert, Mr. Jacobsen read the whole story aloud. He said he was proud of me. I felt puffed up all that afternoon. As I pedaled up Main Street at the end of the workday, I was thinking that my mom had probably bought extra copies of the paper to send to my grandmothers and my aunts. Someone would put a copy of the article on the bulletin board at the back of the church.

"Hey, Silly Willy," Barry shouted from the sidewalk in front of the drugstore. "You the goof who had his picture taken with Fatso and the Crip?"

I didn't answer. If I had, I'd have shouted at Barry. I might even have called him "Gnat," which had to be just as hurtful as the names Clive called me.

That night when I was in bed, I thought about friendships. I'd been in Plaintown for almost a year, and I still didn't have a gang of friends like my four Topeka buddies. Jim had a gang of Mennonite farmers to eat with. He probably went fishing with them, and camping. It hurt to think of Jim camping with some other kid.

Then there was Clive and the gang of guys who swarmed around him. I wondered if any of them liked him or if they just liked his rec room. He called Barry "the Gnat," but I never heard nasty names for his other friends. Maybe he was a better friend than I had imagined. Still, he was a braggart, and he looked like a slug, and he called me "Silly Willy Four-Eyes" and "Brat." I did not like Clive. I would never like him.

Chapter 14

For Kansas kids, nothing except Christmas beats the county fair. The 1942 county fair in Plaintown wasn't much different from fairs I'd been to when we'd lived in Topeka and when we'd visited my grandparents in Oklahoma. Every fair has a midway with a Ferris wheel and a merry-go-round for little kids and old people, plus heart-stopping rides for people like me who want to be scared. There is always a fun house, and there are games promising wonderful prizes that only a few people ever win.

Animals, many of them raised by 4-H kids hoping to win blue ribbons, are on display. Inside buildings or tents are booths sponsored by the churches and clubs and political parties. There are long tables of pickles and pies and quilts.

What was different this year in Plaintown was the war bond booth in the main building. Veterans of the

World War, and one old man from the Spanish-American War, sold bonds and stamps from the center of a table draped with red, white, and blue crepe paper. Three of our planes were displayed on each end of the table. Above the booth a banner read, SUPPORT OUR FINE YOUNG MEN. BUY BONDS. Beneath the banner were pictures of every person in our county who was currently serving in one of the armed forces. In the center, framed in black, were the pictures of three who had died.

In spite of gas rationing, many people drove to the fair from neighboring towns. Allen had to work at the gas station most of the weekend of the fair, but Danny, Dwight, or I planned to be at the booth as often as possible to answer questions about our models and to see that no one damaged them.

Friday afternoon I tended the booth while Dwight pushed Danny's wheelchair through all of the animal exhibits. Friday evening I pushed Danny through the crowds at the midway. We stopped to watch the little kids on the merry-go-round; otherwise, I hurried past most of the rides. I figured that it must hurt Danny not to be able to try them himself.

We stopped to watch the ring toss and the duck shoot. One of the games was something that looked like a giant thermometer with a bell on top. Below the thermometer was a pad and a hammer the size of an ax. When you hit the pad with the hammer, a disk ran up the thermometer, and if you hit hard enough, the disk would go all the way to the top and ring the bell. The prize for ringing the bell was a big teddy bear. Of course you had to pay to try.

Danny and I watched one young man fail, and then Mr. Jacobsen came by, paid his money, and picked up the hammer. He balanced it in his hands, swung it a few times, and then raised it high and banged it down on the pad. The disk went up and up and up, and fell just as I was beginning to think it would make it all the way to the bell. Mr. Jacobsen turned, saw me, and winked. "Not bad for an old man," he said.

A huge, broad kid who had played center on the football team stepped up, paid his money, picked up the hammer and, without any preliminary balancing or swinging, raised it, lowered it—and won the teddy bear. Everyone clapped.

And then Jim Reimer picked up the hammer. I remembered how he had carried two boxes of heavy books when we'd moved in. Now, a year later, he was even taller and probably stronger. Still, I couldn't believe that he could do what Mr. Jacobsen couldn't do. For one thing, he was too skinny. Others must have been as doubtful as me.

"Save your money, kid," a man in the crowd yelled. "That's a man's test, not a boy's."

"Save your money, kid," another voice repeated— Barry's voice.

Jim swung the hammer a few times as silence filled the space around us. Then he lifted it high and lowered it squarely on the pad. The disk climbed the thermometer up and up and . . . I held my breath . . . a foot more and it would reach the bell. It fell back. Everyone in the crowd sighed as they watched the disk fall. Then they clapped. Jim grinned; his eyes sparkled beneath his mismatched eyebrows.

As he walked through the crowd, I was reaching out to touch his shoulder when I remembered the anger between us on the day I'd paid Mr. Schultz. Our eyes met; neither of us spoke. A dark cloth of sadness dropped over me.

Saturday afternoon, after a hair-raising ride on the Loop-the-Loop, I headed to the main building to take over so that Dwight could push the wheelchair to the grandstand for the horse races.

"Some of your friends were just here," Dwight said. "Barry made it sound like he'd done most of the work on these planes. I asked if he wanted to man the booth for a few hours. He didn't." Dwight laughed and pushed Danny out through the building.

I stepped behind the counter and straightened the models. When I looked up I saw Jim leaning against a post, eating cotton candy. I didn't smile. Neither did he. I turned away when an old couple came to the booth. The man pointed to our B-36. "See, Mother, that's the plane our George is flying. Somewhere. Wherever." He shook his shoulders as if to put the memory of his son flying that plane out of his mind. "Did you make some of these?" he asked me.

"Actually, I worked on five of them. The others

made this one while I was driving a tractor during the harvest."

"Such good boys, to work so hard when other boys your age are enjoying their vacations." The lady patted my hand.

"We'll just step up and express our gratitude," the man said as he took bills out of his pocket and bought a bond.

Jim was still standing near the post–with Anne Armstrong. She was holding his arm with both her hands and looking up into his face while he was looking out over her head. Anne seemed to be pleading with him. Or begging. Jim just shook his head from time to time. *Be nice to her, Jim,* I wanted to shout. What I really wanted to do was leave my post to rush to her side. While I watched, she reached up and patted his cheek and then turned and saw me.

She was smiling brightly, but when she came near I saw tears shining in her eyes. She didn't say "hi" or "hello." She said, "Do you think I'm a bad person, William?"

"No, I do not." No one could think Anne was a bad person. She was beautiful and smart and kind and she sang like a radio star.

"I'd like to write to Phil, but the Reimers won't give me his address. Why do you think that is?"

I shook my head. "Maybe they think you'd influence him so that he would want to go off to war," I suggested. *Maybe because you wear lipstick,* I thought.

"You saw how much influence I had all winter and

spring. I tried to change him then. Now I just want to understand, if that's possible. He's a good Christian, and I'm a good Christian–at least I try to be. Why couldn't we be good Christians together? Because of the war. That's why. I'm just so . . ." She didn't finish whatever she was going to say. Instead, she looked into my eyes and smiled. "So how have you been, William?"

She listened as if what I had to say about my new bike and the money I had earned and working on the models really interested her. I had finally finished talking about me and was beginning to ask about the camp she'd been working at when a cheerleader named Betty Sue entered the exhibit hall and screeched Anne's name. She continued to screech as she ran toward us, telling Anne–and everyone in the building–how much she had missed Anne, how glad she was that Anne was home, and how they'd have to spend hours catching up. Anne patted my cheek– I wished she hadn't patted Jim's cheek, too–and walked off with Betty Sue.

The worst thing about being the preacher's kid is that you're supposed to be "a shining example." I couldn't go to the fair on the last day, Sunday. I was glad to go to church, because Anne Armstrong sang. Besides, the fair didn't open until noon. But to have to stay home all of Sunday afternoon seemed to me to be cruel.

During the sermon I tried to think of a way to change Dad's mind. I wouldn't have to go on any of the rides or do any of the fun stuff. I could just sit at the booth. I presented this argument while we ate our Sunday dinner. Dad stuck to his "no."

We were still at the table when Mr. Herbert phoned and asked me if I would be at the booth soon. When I explained that Dad wouldn't let me come, he asked to speak to my father.

"You may go to the fair, William, to help Mr. Herbert," Dad said when he returned to the table.

I didn't ask what had made Dad change his mind. Instead, I excused myself and ran all the way to the fairgrounds. I wasn't riding my new bike during fair week, afraid it could be stolen with so many strangers in town.

As I walked through the main building to our booth, I saw the backs of Dwight and two of the old veterans. I elbowed my way through the crowd to find out what they were staring at. What I saw made me cry out. Five of our planes had been smashed! I would have liked to have said all the cuss words I knew, but cussing is something else that a preacher's kid can't do. Allen came and stood beside me, silently.

"No sudden breeze or careless arm did this," one of the veterans said. "I can only imagine that some dastardly person or persons put each model on the ground and stomped on it. Who, in our little town, could hate so much?"

"The Mennonites," Dwight whispered. "Mennonite kids won't even stand to sing patriotic songs." He was saying exactly what I was thinking.

My stomach churned as Dwight explained that Mr. Herbert had taken Danny home because he didn't think he was safe and that he was going to pick up five more planes to replace the five we had lost. We would guard our booth until the fair closed that night. Allen had to pump gas for a few hours, but he said he would be back.

The sheriff came by. "Anyone could have done it," he said. The doors of the exhibit hall had been locked at ten o'clock Saturday night and they were still locked at noon when the fair reopened. But the windows had been left open so that the night air could cool the hall. In fact, the ladies reported a dusty footprint on the quilt beneath one window. They had brushed it away immediately. Outside the window was a trash can. A person wouldn't have to be particularly agile to climb onto the can and through the window, onto the quilt and down. Anyone between the ages of six and eighty could have done it, the sheriff said.

The smashed planes told him nothing except that whoever did it was thorough. Five planes had been reduced to splinters. None of us could figure out why one plane was left undamaged.

The sheriff said he was sorry, and turned to leave when Dwight again said what I was thinking: "What about the Mennonites?"

"What about them?" the Sheriff asked.

"They don't want to contribute to the war effort in any way," I said.

"So? They don't contribute, but I haven't known

them to destroy what others are doing. Is there anything here that points to the Mennonites?"

Not directly, I thought, but Jim had been standing right by that post watching the booth and the old couple who bought a bond to "support Plaintown's fine young men."

Mr. Herbert returned with five more models, and we set them in place. I had scratched a tiny "w" under the wing on every plane made mostly by me. I hadn't made any of the six now on display.

Monday morning, I rode out to Jim Reimer's. I spoke nicely to his family, but as soon as I had Jim alone I turned and let him see the full force of my anger. I clenched my fists and shook one in his face. "So why did you do it?" I demanded.

"Do what?" Jim looked confused, but he didn't fool me.

"You know darn well what you did. You destroyed five of our model planes. All five of them were made mostly by me, as you must have noticed. You care more about people in Germany than you care about people in your own country. You are"—I couldn't think of a strong enough word—"You are despicable," I shouted as I mounted my bike.

"I did not touch your planes, William." He spoke slowly and clearly without shouting. I didn't believe him.

Chapter 15

During the last weeks of summer, I continued to work on the planes, and at the Jacobsens'. I also learned to make a hamburger casserole and a pork chop dinner. Darlene learned to make a tuna fish casserole and macaroni and cheese. Maggie learned to tear up lettuce for a salad and to set the table. Last spring all five of us had spent every Saturday morning cleaning house. Now Mom had decided that we should also start cooking.

Boys mow lawns and clean garages. In the winter they shovel snow. Sometimes they fix things. They do not scrub kitchen floors and they do not cook. That's what I told Mom. She told me that these were unusual times and that everyone had to do his part. She couldn't–or she wouldn't–understand that "my part" was making model planes, not cooking supper.

Mom also said that most of the famous chefs are men, as if I cared.

I sometimes thought that I had liked Mom better in the old days, when she was sweet and shy and didn't ask so much of me. Darlene wasn't any happier than I was. Only Maggie thought it was "fun" to dust the tops of the furniture and tear up lettuce.

Although kids are supposed to hate school, my sisters and Mom went off happily on the first day of the new school year. So did I.

The new year was very different from the previous year. School days were longer and vacations were fewer and shorter so that more young men could graduate before they went to war. The football season was canceled because our coach had been drafted, several of our best players were already in one or the other of the services, and gas rationing made it difficult for teams to travel. Without football we had no need for a marching band.

In the winter we would have a basketball team, although the intramural schedule would be shortened. That was good news for Allen, who might make first string. I wished that I could try out for the team, but I was still several inches too short.

Two afternoons a week I went to Mr. Herbert's after school. Other afternoons, when the weather was okay, I went to the school yard to help Allen get in shape for basketball practice which would begin in November. I was a reporter for the school paper, and I was skipping study hall in order to take an extra science course. I was also cleaning and cooking and going to church four times on Sundays. I went to the picture show most Saturday afternoons.

I could have gone to Clive's on Friday nights. Clive actually invited me, in his own obnoxious way: "Hey, Silly Willy, I've decided to let you come to my house tonight. Seven o'clock."

Allen went to Clive's on Friday nights. I would have gone if it hadn't meant kowtowing to Clive. "Thanks but no thanks," I said as I turned and walked away.

Then, early in October, Chester's plane was shot down in the South Pacific!

Dad said I had to go to Clive's house. "Clive is your friend. You have no choice but to go and do whatever you can to ease his suffering."

I don't know where he got the idea that Clive was my friend, but that wasn't the time to tell him that Clive was really my enemy.

The Van Dyne house was stone with a circular driveway. Clive's aunt, Mrs. Busybody Van Goose and her husband, Banker Van Dyne, lived in a brick house next door, but she was at the Elevator Van Dyne house that afternoon. She opened the big carved door before Dad rang the bell, and led us through a dark, cavernous hallway to the living room. Clive and his father sat on either side of Clive's mother on one of the two sofas. His mother was crying. Although the room was full of people, there was no other sound. Clive's aunt directed me to a chair next to the end of the sofa where Clive was sitting.

As I sat down, Clive looked at me and glared. That was a surprise. I'd expected him to be so sad about his brother that he wouldn't notice me. All of a sudden he stood up, pointed to the ceiling, and stomped out of the room. At the doorway he stopped.

What was I supposed to do? I looked at my father, who motioned to me to follow Clive. As soon as I stood up, Clive started running up the stairs. I walked up after him, feeling as lost as if I were in a jungle. I stopped for just a minute to admire the stained-glass window on the landing, and then I went on up to a wide hall. I turned left, which is the direction Clive had turned, and passed closed doors until I found Clive lying facedown on the bed in a room which I assumed was his until I realized how neat it was. The rug in front of the bed was perfectly flat and straight. The dresser top was bare except for a few framed pictures. A whole row of trophies stood on top of bookshelves. *Trophies?*

"Your brother won a lot of trophies," I said, and began to read them off. "Spelling bee, most valuable player on the baseball team, basketball, track, and another for baseball."

"I don't have any trophies," Clive muttered into the pillow.

"He was older," I said aloud. *And probably nicer,* I thought.

Clive didn't say anything for a long time.

"You must be feeling crummy," I whispered.

"Yeah." Suddenly he sat up and glared at me again. "I hate him," he said. "Hate him. When he graduated from high school, he could have gone to any college. Even Princeton. That's what my folks wanted him to do. My uncle went to Princeton. But, no, Mr. U.S.A. said that America couldn't stay out of the war much longer. He said he wanted to be ready to do his part. So the day after he graduated from high school, he joined up."

"He was right about the war," I murmured.

"Yeah. He was right about everything. My folks thought he was the next thing to Jesus Christ. *'Chester this, Chester that. Why can't you be more like Chester?'* I was going out for football this year. I thought that would make everyone proud of me. So what do they do? They cancel the whole damned season."

"What about basketball or baseball?" I asked. Even as I spoke I realized that Clive might play, but he was too awkward and slow to be a star.

Clive shook his head. "What's so great about going off to get killed? Tell me. What's so great about that? My uncle doesn't have any kids, so Chester was supposed to take over the bank when he grew up. I'd run the elevator. So what am I supposed to do now? Take over the whole town? It's hard enough to be the only Van Dyne in the high school, to have to preserve the Van Dyne heritage." He slammed his fist into a pillow and lay down again.

I stared at him. I couldn't believe what I was hearing. Clive thought it was his *duty* to be the most important kid in our class. He sure had a strange notion of how to go about being a leader, or whatever he thought was involved in "preserving the Van Dyne heritage."

When I didn't say anything, he sat up and pointed his finger at me. "You're a minister's kid. No one expects much of you."

That's what you think. I'm expected to be mannerly, and speak nicely to everyone, and to go to four services every Sunday and to be an example. That's what I thought. I didn't *say* anything.

"Chester made our family proud. I can't do anything as good as he did it." His voice broke into something like a sob. "I sometimes wished he would die," he whispered.

I swallowed once, and swallowed again, shocked. "Your folks would feel just as sad if anything happened to you. I know they would."

"You don't know anything. Go away," he muttered.

I went to the door. "I really am sorry," I said. "You want my dad to come up? Or my mom?"

"I want to be left alone," he said.

I went downstairs. Mom met me in the hall, and we stood together while Dad said, "'Blessed are they that mourn, for they shall be comforted.'" While Dad prayed, I said a silent take-care-of-Clive prayer.

Because I'm a preacher's kid, I've been to more funerals than most adults. Chester's funeral service was different from all of the others. The army hadn't returned his body, so there was a large picture of

Chester in his uniform, but no casket. I was grateful for that. I always stay in my seat while friends and family check out the body in an open casket.

The church was packed for Chester's service on Saturday. When the pews were filled, the ushers brought up chairs from the Sunday school rooms and placed them in the aisles and at the back of the church. Chester's grandparents were there, and aunts and uncles and cousins—and most of the young people who were still in town.

Anne Armstrong came home from college. She sang "Abide with Me." Actually, she sang the first verse until she came to "help of the helpless, O abide with me." She whispered those words. The organist played another verse while Anne just stood there with her head bowed. I thought about how Chester had walked Anne home at Christmastime. Anne opened her mouth at the beginning of the next verse, but nothing came out. She turned to the organist, who started over again while Anne took a breath so deep that I could see her shoulders rise. Then she looked straight out over the heads of the congregation and sang with her usual clear voice.

One thing I liked about the way Anne sang was that you could understand every word. On the last line, "In life and death, O Lord, abide with me," her voice quavered, but she got through it. My grandmother once told me that this was the most comforting hymn in the book; I thought it was the most depressing.

The baseball coach spoke about what a fine young man Chester had been and about how he would be missed. Instead of preaching, my father read one Scripture after another: "In my Father's house are many mansions. . . ." "For now we see through a glass, darkly . . ." He didn't even try to explain how God could have let Chester be killed. We all recited "The Lord is my Shepherd." Dad prayed.

Turning to walk out of the sanctuary, I was surprised to see Jim and Mr. Reimer in the back.

"What are they doing here?" Barry asked.

"Paul Reimer and Chester were good friends," one of our deacons answered. "Paul was the catcher and Chester the pitcher on the baseball team. They won the regional championship that year. I expect that Mr. Reimer and his younger son came because Paul couldn't."

When I got to the church basement, where the ladies were serving coffee and punch and cookies, I looked around for the Reimers, but they were not there.

Clive was standing by the table shoving cookies into his mouth. I went up to him, trying to think what I should say, but he started talking before I opened my mouth. "Why was your friend Jim Reimer here?"

"I think he and his father came because Paul couldn't come."

"Paul's a coward. We don't want him here—or his father or his brother." Clive shouted so that everyone stopped talking and stared. "Cowards!" Clive turned back to the refreshment table and stuffed three more cookies into his mouth.

Barry bounced up and down a few times and then pranced over to look up into Clive's face. "Boy, are you right! All the Reimers are cowards."

"Go away," Clive muttered.

Barry was bewildered. I could see that in his face as he walked toward me. I didn't want to talk to Barry, or Clive, or anybody. I left the church and went home to think.

Chester's death was sad—every serviceman's death is sad—but Chester seemed to have been someone special. A good person. How were good people different from other people? They don't lie or cheat or steal. They care about others. They obey the Commandments. One Commandment is, "Thou shalt not kill." Had Chester killed anyone? Some soldiers must kill, and some must be killed. That's war. But Chester? Someone said that the good die young. Someone else said that life isn't fair. *It sure wasn't fair in Chester's case,* I thought bitterly—*or in Clive's.*

I never had imagined a day when I would pity Clive, but I pitied him then. Bad as it must feel to have your brother die, it must feel worse—atrocious, in fact— if you were jealous of him and had wished him dead, even if you didn't really mean it.

Thinking about Clive, I remembered his threats to *get* me. Had that been his idea of a way to earn my respect? Was he trying to prove that he could be the leader of the freshmen class just as his father and uncle were leaders of the town? Was he stupid? He was a "B" or "C" sort of student, but you couldn't tell everything from grades. *Poor Clive!*

Clive was in school on Monday. I tried to be friendly. I said, "Hi" and "Did you do your homework?" and "What do you think of the Cards winning the series?" those kinds of dumb things. Clive never bothered to respond.

Friday afternoon Allen said that Clive's dad had told Allen's dad that he hoped the boys would come to play Ping-Pong and pool that night as usual. Allen asked me to come, too.

So I went. It was a neat rec room, paneled in dark wood with big sofas and tables and a record player and the Ping-Pong table and a pool table. There were Cokes and root beer. Clive sat in the corner most of the evening. When I went to sit with him, he let me jabber about the World Series and nodded a couple of times so I knew he was listening.

Chapter 16

The Saturday movie was *Paris Calling,* about members of the French underground who were destroying the Nazis who had taken over their country. I wished, for Clive's sake, that it had not been about war. But it was exciting, one of those movies that left me feeling exhilarated, like I could slay the enemy with a single blow. That's what makes movies so great. Mom says that Ginger Rogers-Fred Astaire movies always make her feel that she can dance, until she tries a few spins and kicks.

After the movie, while we were standing in front of the Roxy waiting for our eyes to adjust to bright sunlight, Jim came out of the drugstore across the street. I saw him, but my thoughts were still with the fearless French in Paris.

"Hey, *Junge* Jim," Clive shouted as we crossed the street. "We want to talk to you." Jim stood like a tree with its roots planted in the sidewalk while Clive twisted the neck of Jim's sweater up against his throat.

When Clive said, "Move," five of us together pulled and pushed Jim into the alley next to the drug-store and down the alley past the garbage cans. At the end of the alley, we pinned Jim against a wooden fence with his arms outstretched.

Clive slapped his cheek. "That's in memory of my brother," Clive said. "My brother who died for his country, my only brother."

"Yeah," we all shouted together. I was still picturing myself as a fearless member of the French under-ground.

Jim turned the other cheek. Clive slapped it so that Jim had matching red splotches on either side of his nose. We laughed.

"Why'd you go to Chester's funeral?" Clive asked.

"Chester was Paul's friend," Jim whispered. "We went to show our sympathy for your family."

"Sympathy? You think we want sympathy from a family of cowards?"

"And traitors," I added, thinking of my smashed planes.

Jim said nothing.

"If your brother cared about Chester, he'd be out there helping with the fight, not hiding in some nice, clean hospital handing out aspirin tablets." Clive socked Jim in the stomach, hard. "That's for all the other brave soldiers who aren't afraid to die."

"And that," Tom and John snarled together as they

pulled Jim away from the fence and twisted his arms.

Clive knocked Jim to the ground and sat on him. "Is Phil having fun playing in the dirt with all those other goof-offs?" Clive punched him again. "Are you ashamed of your brothers, Jim?"

Jim shook his head, but still he did not speak.

"Answer the question," I shouted as I kicked Jim in the ribs.

Jim turned and looked straight into my eyes. I jumped away until my back was hard against the brick wall of the drugstore. I bit down on the back of my hand to keep myself from making a strangled noise.

Clive was red in the face, and he and Tom and John and Barry were all on their knees pummeling Jim's bleeding body. I watched, no longer elevated by the bravery of the underground, but paralyzed with horror. When Clive began to lift Jim's shoulders, I sprang forward.

"Stop," I shouted as I thrust my hand under Jim's head. My knuckles crashed into the cement, and pain darted up my arm and brought tears to my eyes.

"What's going on here?" someone shouted. The other boys scrambled over the fence into the next street.

I was on my knees next to Jim. I stood up. I wanted to run, but I couldn't. Someone helped Jim to his feet. His face was bloody, and his sweater was in shreds; he moved as if every bone in his body throbbed as much as my hand. My hand! It didn't look like a hand at all but more like a hunk of white bread streaked with grape jelly. My stomach churned, and black clouds passed across my eyes.

The first time I came to, I was hanging over a shoulder with my head at belt level. A sidewalk was passing quickly beneath the feet of the man who was carrying me. The druggist was running along behind us holding a box to support my hand. Neither seemed to hear me when I tried to say that I could walk.

When he lowered me to the white table in the doctor's office, I saw that the man carrying me was Mr. Jacobsen. The doctor gave me a shot. I must have been out for quite a while, because when I opened my eyes again, both my parents were in the room and my hand was strapped to a board with wide strips of gauze.

"Believe me, we appreciate what you've done," Mr. Reimer said as he walked toward me. I had pushed Jim into an alley and kicked him. I'd called him a traitor. How could he appreciate that? "If you hadn't cushioned Jim's head, he'd have had a concussion—or worse. You're a Good Samaritan, William, and a good Christian."

I tried to speak, to tell Mr. Reimer that he had it all wrong. I was anything *but* a good Christian.

Mr. Reimer patted my shoulder—my other shoulder. "Don't try to talk, son. We'll continue this conversation in a few days. In the meantime, you'll want to know that your friend Jim is going to be fine—just lots of bruises."

If I had spoken, I would have howled, so I turned my head away.

The doctor came back into the room and helped me sit up. Then my parents helped me out to the car.

Sunday morning my hand still hurt, but not a lot except when I moved it. The doctor had said that some of the little bones were probably broken; he couldn't tell for sure until the swelling went down. In the meantime, when I wasn't soaking my hand, it had to be strapped to the splint and carried in a sling.

I had been in bed since late Saturday afternoon and I wanted to stay there forever. When I didn't come down to breakfast, Mom brought me an eggnog and two pieces of toast.

"Are you still feeling woozy?" She frowned. "I know your hand hurts. Maybe you'd better stay home from Sunday school. If you feel like going to church, you can come over later."

I didn't feel like going anyplace; I didn't feel like getting out of bed. I didn't feel like eating either.

She stood looking down at me. And then she spoke in her tough-Mom voice. "Sit up and eat your breakfast. If you feel weak, it's because you refused dinner." She stood there until I obeyed.

When the glass and plate were empty and I was lying back on my pillow, she sighed and left the room. "Don't forget to soak your hand," she called from the stairway.

I didn't *forget* to soak my hand, I just didn't do it. I got up once to go to the bathroom and went back to bed without brushing my teeth. My arms and legs felt like weights. A lump as big as a basketball filled my chest.

I spent the morning staring at my ceiling while I tried to push every ugly thought and scene out of my brain. I couldn't. I kept seeing the five of us pushing Jim into that alley. Five of us had done it: Clive and Tom and John and Barry and I. Not Allen. He had been at the movies with us, but he hadn't even crossed the street. Had he known something ugly was about to happen? Why hadn't I gone away with him? Jim might have been hurt worse. So why hadn't the two of us, Allen and I, stopped the others? Were we as bad as the German people who let the Nazis torture the Jews?

One thing I did know: Clive was wrong when he called Jim Reimer a coward. I knew for sure that Jim was brave. I had seen him run right in front of a charging bull. His brothers probably would have done the same thing. I could not believe that Phil was refusing to put on a uniform or that Paul was refusing to carry a gun because they were *afraid* to fight.

Jim had stood beside me during my first days in Plaintown. He had prevented Clive from clobbering me. And what had I done? I had *helped* Clive beat and bloody Jim. I had also called Jim a traitor because he had smashed my model planes. *Are you sure he smashed your planes?* a little voice whispered. Of course he smashed my planes. Who else would have done it? No, I should not have kicked Jim. But he had smashed my planes . . . *He said he didn't.*

• • •

"How many times have you soaked your hand?" Mom asked when she came upstairs to change out of her church dress. I shook my head; she glared at me. "Get up and go downstairs. Fill the dishpan with warm water and keep your hand in it until dinner is on the table."

She went downstairs, but I didn't move. I couldn't. I heard the screen door bang as Dad came in and announced that the girls were going to have dinner with the Bush sisters, two old ladies who made a big fuss over Darlene and Maggie and often invited them for dinner after church.

Except for the barest murmur of voices, I heard nothing from downstairs for several minutes. Then I heard two sets of footsteps on the stairs, and Mom and Dad were standing over my bed.

"What's the matter?" Dad asked.

I turned on my side with my face to the wall.

"We know your hand hurts. Soaking will help it. You may also have more aspirin." He waited for me to say something, but I didn't.

"Do you hurt anyplace else? Do you feel sick?" Mom put her hand on my forehead to check for fever.

"Mr. Reimer phoned this morning to ask about you," Dad said. "He said his congregation would be thanking God for your brave act."

Brave act, indeed. I shut my eyes tight to hold in the tears. "Leave me alone," I muttered.

"What is going on, William?" Mom asked in her I'm-so-tired voice.

I didn't answer. How could I?

In the silence I sensed that Dad and Mom were speaking in their eye-to-eye language. Then I heard Mom leave the room. "I'll hold dinner," she said.

Dad sat down on the side of the bed. "Turn over and look at me, William." I turned, but I carefully looked past him to the plane hanging above my dresser. "Something is very wrong. It must have something to do with Mr. Reimer's gratitude, but I know you too well to think that you are so modest that you can't stand a little praise. . . ."

He waited a long time for me to speak. I had nothing to say. Finally he sighed. "Perhaps you feel that you don't deserve the praise. Is that it? Was your hand not under Jim's head? Or was it there for some other purpose?"

I shook my head. I had meant to protect Jim's head. That was the least I could do after I had helped push him into the alley and then kicked him.

"If you are not sick and you did protect Jim's head, what is the matter with you? Answer me. Now." Dad was angry.

"I kicked Jim," I whispered as I turned onto my stomach and covered my head with my pillow. "Before that, I helped push him into the alley. I called him a traitor."

After more long minutes of silence, Dad stood up and lifted a corner of the pillow. "I'll call Mr. Reimer and tell him you don't deserve his thanks and praise. I'll leave it to you to set things right with Jim. Remember,

William, the words of the psalmist, who said, 'The Lord is nigh unto them that are of a broken heart; and saveth such as be of a contrite spirit.' Now get up and feed your stomach so you'll have strength to deal with your contrite spirit."

At the door he turned. "Incidentally, William, you're grounded until after Thanksgiving. The young hoodlums you call friends should be grounded, too. How many brave young men did it take to fell one? Who were they?" While I was trying to think how to answer that question, Dad withdrew it. "Never mind, William. I won't ask you to tattle, though no boy who was in that alley yesterday afternoon deserves your protection, whether he actually participated or not. Thank God you came to your senses before Jim Reimer was seriously hurt."

Damn it. Did my dad add that last sentence just to make me feel worse?

I ate Sunday dinner with my parents. They talked about the sermon and the music and who was in church and whether old Mrs. Bradford was looking more frail and who they could find to teach the older elementary age Sunday school class.

I said nothing, but I ate. Actually, I was hungry. Thank goodness it was my left hand that was hurt! I read the funnies while I soaked my hand. Then I did my geometry homework and read the assigned pages of *The Merchant of Venice* while I soaked my hand again.

I didn't have any choice about going to youth

group that evening. If asked, I would have chosen to stay home, especially when Dad announced that we— not I, but Dad and I—would be exactly five minutes late. I knew then that it was not going to be the usual meeting, and I feared what Dad might do or say. I was right to fear.

The noise in the room dropped to silence as we entered. I slunk into the chair nearest to the door while Dad strode to the front of the room.

"I am here to speak directly to whomever had any part in the attack on Jim Reimer yesterday afternoon. I don't know who you were—except for William, of course. How many of you did it take to knock down one boy? Five? Six? Once you had him down, how many of you hit and kicked him?"

Dad was silent, staring into the faces of each of us, for what seemed to be minutes. Then slowly he opened his Bible and began to read: "'Ye have heard that it hath been said, An eye for an eye, and a tooth for a tooth: But I say unto you, That ye resist not evil: but whosoever shall smite thee on thy right cheek, turn to him the other also.'"

"Jim turned the other cheek," I muttered, wishing even as I heard my voice that I had kept silent.

"Did he?" Dad smiled, obviously pleased. "What does that say about Jim Reimer?" He looked around from face to face, waiting for an answer. He did not look at me, for which I was grateful; I didn't want to be Goody Two Shoes.

Finally, Mary Ellen spoke. "Jim is a good Christian."

"A better Christian than many of us, wouldn't you say?"

Several kids nodded.

"His brothers won't fight for their country," Clive said. "My brother—"

"Maybe you think Jim is your enemy," Dad interrupted Clive. "I wouldn't agree, but you all know what Jesus said about loving your enemy and doing good to them that hate you, though I don't think Jim hates you." Dad chuckled. "He may, however, be having trouble thinking kindly of some of you when he tries to move his sore body today. The point is that you who profess to be Christians, who have been confirmed into our church, have behaved like a pack of bullies, while he turned the other cheek."

Dad went on to talk about the Mennonites and how they had been persecuted in one country after another because they would not send their young men to war.

"But they let other young men do their fighting for them. I read that Hitler was sending Jews to camps where they are thrown into ovens and burned to death. Do the Mennonites think that's okay?" That question came from Tom.

"I'm sure they do not think it is okay. I've talked to pacifists about that. They think that war—all war—is wrong, and that there is a better way to handle differences. They believe that if you are a Christian you must obey the Bible, not just the parts that you agree with. Many pacifists are already making plans for the time of healing that will follow this war. They will be there to bind the wounds of our enemies as well as of our friends. The Mennonites also believe that they have a special calling to try to demonstrate that it is possible to follow all of the teachings of Christ."

Dad prayed for Jim and his family and for the boys who had done "this great wrong." Then he prayed for understanding and tolerance.

When he had finished praying, he walked to the door, motioning me to go out ahead of him. At the door, he turned. "William has been grounded until Thanksgiving. I don't know if there will be punishment for the rest of you or not. That is not my business."

Chapter 17

Monday morning Barry was waiting for me on the sidewalk in front of our house. "So, William, you're grounded." He punched me on the shoulder. Later he shouted to Clive and Tom across the street, "Here's old Silly Willy. We won't be seeing much of him in the next few weeks. No more picture shows. No more shooting baskets after school. If it turns cold, we'll all be sledding or ice-skating–except the Preacher's Brat. Poor William!"

Barry may have thought he was funny; I didn't. I turned away from him and hurried on. Clive and Tom crossed the street, and I could hear their footsteps behind me.

"Wait up, William. Please," Clive called. I stood still while he walked up beside me. "Your hand hurt much?" he asked. I shook my head. "Thanks for not ratting on us," he said.

"Yeah, thanks," Tom muttered.

Clive, Tom, and Barry hurried on ahead. I stood staring at their backs. Clive had said *thank you*. Who would believe it?

I thought about Barry's reaction to my being grounded. He should have been grounded, too. Barry was an A-plus pain in the neck. He said mean things. He had been a nuisance when we were working on the planes. I thought about the planes that had been smashed.

After lunch, Allen drew me to a corner of the lunchroom. "I made a big mistake when I walked away from what I thought might be a fight Saturday. You and I together could have stopped it before it began. I'm sorry I let you down, William. And Jim. I sure let him down."

He turned away before I had a chance to answer him. I was glad, because I never did figure out what I should have said. I couldn't say, *I forgive you*. I didn't have anything to forgive him for.

Barry was ahead of me as we left the school that afternoon, but I called to him, and he waited and bounced along beside me, chattering as usual. I let him chatter. I don't think he noticed that I said absolutely nothing. We walked around my house to the backyard. He looked up at me, surprised, when I did not go to my back door but continued crunching through the fallen leaves until we were almost to the alley.

"I want to ask you one question," I said. "Did you smash the planes at the fair?"

"Wh-what planes?" he asked as his face turned

bright pink, which answered my question as well as any words.

"You did, didn't you? Why?"

He turned and ran into the alley.

I ran after him and pulled him back with my right arm wrapped around his neck. "You're not getting out of here until you answer me."

"Why should I answer you?"

"Because I'm bigger than you and I have you in a lock hold, and I won't let go until you start talking."

When he nodded, I released his neck but I rested my bandaged left hand on his shoulder. "The five planes that were smashed were mine. Did you choose them because I made them?" I couldn't believe that, but still . . .

"Yeah." He hung his head, and his voice was a whisper. "You give me a pain, Silly Willy Four-Eyes. Everybody thinks your dad is so great. *Reverend Spencer says, Reverend Spencer does.* He prays at the train station and he stands up there with the mayor." As he spoke, Barry's voice grew louder. "You're just like him. Everybody thinks you're a great kid. Mr. Jacobsen's known me since I was a baby, but it's *you* he asks to help him. *You* get a fancy new bike. *You* start growing. *You* get your picture in the paper, and *you* think you're better than anybody else. Clive says you're a snob. He's right about that." He twisted away from me and ran.

I let him go. What was there for me to say? That my dad wasn't a good man? I had often wondered about Barry's father. Was he never coming home? I couldn't deny that Mr. Jacobsen has asked me to work on the farm, or that I had grown, or that my picture had been in the paper. How could *anyone* think I was a snob? I was a lonely guy who wanted friends. I just didn't want friends like Clive and Barry.

Enough whining. I ran to the house and into the kitchen. "Where's Dad?" I shouted as I ran into the kitchen.

"Over at the church, I expect," Mom said. "You haven't had your snack. Are you okay?"

I nodded. I would have been okay if I hadn't been grounded. I begged Mom to let me go to the church. She looked surprised, but agreed.

"I've got to get out to the Reimers'," I shouted to Dad as I ran up the stairs to his office. "Please drive me. It's important."

"It can't wait until tomorrow?"

"No, Dad. It can't. And even if I weren't grounded, I couldn't ride out there on my bike."

"I see," he said when I held up my splinted hand. "You couldn't phone?"

"It's private." Everyone knows that party telephone lines make it impossible to say anything on the phone that you don't want the whole town to hear.

Without another word, Dad got up from his desk and turned off the light. He waved to Mom in the kitchen window as we shuffled through the leaves to the garage.

Mr. Reimer and his daughters were in the barn, getting ready to milk. Jim wasn't with them, so I went to the house. Mrs. Reimer greeted me warmly–maybe she didn't know that I had kicked her son–and told me to go on through to the dining room. Jim was sitting in front of the stove.

I gasped when he turned toward me. The skin around his comic eyebrow was black, green, and purple. His eye was half closed. His lip was split, so that he grimaced when he grinned.

"Does your body look as bad as your face?"

"Worse." He laughed. "Some people are white, some are brown, and I am multicolored."

I squatted down in front of him. "I'm sorry," I said, "for accusing you of smashing my planes."

"How do you know I didn't?"

"Because I know who did." I decided not to tell him it was Barry. "And I'm sorry about Saturday after-noon."

"Sorry you protected my head?" He pointed to my bandaged hand. "Hurt much?"

"Not much. You know what I'm sorry about. I'm sorry I pushed and kicked you and for what I said. Really sorry. I behaved like a thug. I don't know why." I shook my head. "I think I was hypnotized by the movie I had just seen. But that's not an excuse. Allen went to the same movie and he didn't push you into the alley. You and Phil saved me from Clive. I know that, whatever Clive says, you are def-initely not a coward. You might not fight people, but you'd have fought that bull if you'd had to. And I have been–"

"That's enough apology, too much. I don't think I would ever hit you or any person, but I don't know that for sure. Sometimes we get caught up. Remember that first assembly after Pearl Harbor? I listened to all that rousing music and when I heard the words about standing up if we were willing to support the war effort, you saw what I did. I stood up. I was saying–for that moment–that I would do something that is against my religion, my family, everything we believe. Right after I stood up, I sat down. Right after you kicked me, you protected my head." He laughed. "Too bad we didn't have our right thoughts *before* our wrong ones."

While he was still talking, I was thinking, *What a neat guy!* He could have been so sanctimonious. But he wasn't.

"Thanks," was all I could think to say. We sat silently for a long time. "I've missed you," I muttered at last.

He grinned. "We could have been great friends." More silence. "How you getting along with Clive?"

"Okay. Actually, I feel sorry for Clive. He thinks that his family is the most important family in Plaintown, and that it is somehow his duty to be the most important kid in the high school. He also thinks I'm a snob."

Jim laughed to show that *he* didn't think I was a snob. "His brother was different. He and Paul were more than just baseball buddies. Paul really admired Chester." He sighed. "Chester wasn't a bully, that's for sure. But I guess you're right. We should feel sorry for Clive. I've seen you with Allen. He's okay. Is he your pal?"

I thought and then grinned. "Yeah, I guess he is, but he doesn't have a crazy eyebrow. And there's a kid named Dwight, a junior. And a freshman named Danny."

"And Barry?"

"Not Barry," I said. "And you?"

Jim told me about his friends and about Dorothy. Jim had a thing for Dorothy. I remembered how she stood up when the teacher had asked if she would bring in scrap metal, and I nodded my approval.

When I asked him about his brothers, he said they hadn't heard from Paul in a long time. "In September he was in England. We hope he's not in Africa now. We don't know."

"The Allies won at El Alamein. We're pushing the Axis troops back."

Jim nodded. "And lots of men on both sides are wounded and dead. Paul is driving an ambulance, somewhere."

"He wouldn't have time to write if he's working on a battlefield." I hoped he was too busy, not too wounded. "How's Phil?"

"Phil is bored. There isn't enough work for them to do yet. He's hoping to get reassigned to a hospital or a mental institution, someplace where his work will be really valuable."

"Can't he choose?" I asked.

"No. He can't."

Deciding that it was better to move away from that subject, I asked Jim when he thought he'd be back in school and if he wanted me to bring his homework assignments to him. He said he'd be back in a week, and his cousin was bringing the homework. We didn't seem to have anything else to say to one another.

I was glad when I heard the footsteps and bangs that meant the milking was over. "Dad's waiting," I said. "Hope your beautiful colors will fade soon."

"They will. Thank you for coming, William."

"Thank *you* for–everything."

"Did it go well?" Dad asked when he had driven out of the Reimers' lane.

"I guess so." I sat and thought. "Friendship is very complicated, isn't it? When you get older and when there's a war on. Remember Jack and George and Pinky and Pete?"

"Your buddies in Topeka."

"We just played together and tried to build a fort, and sometimes we fought and then we made up. We didn't worry about what was right and what was wrong. We didn't even think about what was going on across town, let alone across the country. Everything was so simple."

"'When I was a child, I spake as a child, I understood as a child, I thought as a child–'"

I interrupted Dad to continue the quotation "'But when I became a man, I put away childish things.'"

"You're becoming a man, William."

Jim Reimer returned to school the following Monday. I spoke to him during gym. Later I asked if

172

he'd finished *The Merchant of Venice.* My attempts to be friendly were feeble.

I haven't done enough, I said to myself as I sat down and opened my lunch bag. I closed the bag and climbed back over the bench.

"Where are you going?" Clive asked.

"To eat with my friend Jim Reimer," I said.

"How can you? He smashed your model planes."

I stood tall and spoke loudly so that everyone in the lunchroom would hear. "Jim Reimer did not smash the planes at the fair. Of that I am absolutely, positively certain."

"So who did?" Clive asked.

I looked at Barry, who was staring up at me with his mouth open as if he were gasping for his last breath. "The guy who did it knows, and I know, and that's enough."

I walked across the lunchroom in complete silence. When I reached the Mennonite table, Jim moved over to make room for me. As I sat down I saw Allen approaching the table. One of the Mennonites got up to make room for him. Another got up to make room for Dwight, who was coming from the table where the juniors ate.

We opened our lunch bags. When we had finished our sandwiches, Jim gave me half of a huge oatmeal cookie. Other kids at the table shared with Allen and Dwight.

No one made any fine speeches about brotherhood or forgiveness or tolerance, but at the end of the meal we shook hands with one another. The next noon hour

I ate at my usual table with Allen and Clive and Tom and John–and Barry. The war was still a wall between the Mennonites and the rest of us, but I could see over the wall.

If I were to discuss the situation with my dad, this is the verse he would quote: "For now we see through a glass, darkly; but then face to face: now I know in part; but then shall I know even as also I am known."

Postscript

This afternoon, May 24, 1945, I will graduate from Plaintown High School. President Roosevelt has died. The war in Europe is over, and we are pushing toward Tokyo in the Pacific. It has been a long, rotten war. Five young men from Plaintown have been killed. Don Jacobsen and several others are missing in action. One came home with a hook replacing the hand that had been blown away.

A camp for Germans prisoners was built right here in Kansas. Some of them were sent out from the camp to work on farms. Two came to help harvest the wheat at the Jacobsens'. Once I saw "the enemy," I could no longer think of them as evil beasts. These two Germans were just a few years older than me. They were little kids when the Nazis began their brutal campaign. The prisoners were good workers who smiled a lot and were trying to learn English. On the last day, they were singing as they walked in from the field. The tune was "A Mighty Fortress Is Our God." I joined in, and it didn't matter that we were singing in two different languages.

The cost of the war was very high for everyone, but this is supposed to be the last war anyone will ever fight. Representatives of fifty nations are meeting in San Francisco to write a charter for a worldwide organization to be called the United Nations. It will settle disputes among countries in the future.

After the battle fought in the Plaintown alley in 1942, I never again experienced that great surge of happy patriotism that my father kept trying to curb. I don't know if Jim Reimer's way is the right way, but I do know that without raising a fist, he shamed me and four other bullies. I now have a crooked little finger to remind me of that day—and of my friend with the crooked eyebrow.

Jim will not be at our graduation. He rushed through high school and earned his diploma in January. He is now working at a mental hospital in Illinois. I went to the train station to see him off. His brother Paul was there on crutches and looking very pale. His ambulance had been strafed, and he was sent home to recuperate.

I was the only non-Mennonite at the station that day. As the train pulled out, I felt an arm around my shoulder and looked up into Mr. Reimer's blue eyes. He nodded and smiled, but he didn't say anything. Neither did I. What could we say?

Barry won't be at graduation either. He stayed away from me for the rest of the sophomore year and moved to California the next summer. I still don't like Clive, but I don't hate him either. I no longer need a pack of buddies, just a few good friends like Allen–and Mary Ellen. I took her to the prom. Dwight has been in the army for more than a year now. Anne Armstrong is married to an army officer and living in Georgia.

My family will be leaving Plaintown next month. Dad will become the minister of a big church in Wichita. Some of the members of that congregation complained to the bishop after Mom announced that she is not a traditional minister's wife and will continue to teach school. We, and the bishop, know that the church people will quickly learn to love her.

My sisters think it will be great to live in a city instead of a little town, but the parsonage in Wichita will never be home to me. I will be attending Ohio Wesleyan in the fall–if I'm not drafted. If I am drafted, I will go to college later. I don't know what I will do with my life. I'd like to think that there is something I can do to help guarantee peace. Perhaps I will feel a call to the ministry, like my dad.

And maybe there will be a day when Jim Reimer and I will take fishing rods to a stream where we will talk together as good friends do. Maybe.